the
summer
i
turned
pretty

Also by Jenny Han
Shug

the
summer
i
turned
pretty

JENNY HAN

Simon & Schuster Books for Young Readers
New York   London   Toronto   Sydney

SIMON & SCHUSTER BOOKS FOR YOUNG READERS
An imprint of Simon & Schuster Children's Publishing Division
1230 Avenue of the Americas, New York, New York 10020

SIMON & SCHUSTER BOOKS FOR YOUNG READERS is a trademark of Simon & Schuster, Inc.
Book design by Lucy Ruth Cummins
The text for this book is set in Bembo.
Manufactured in the United States of America
10 9 8 7 6 5 4 3 2 1
Library of Congress Cataloging-in-Publication Data
Han, Jenny.
The summer I turned pretty / Jenny Han.—1st ed.
p. cm.
Summary: Belly spends the summer she turns sixteen at the beach just like every other summer of her life, but this time things are very different.
ISBN: 978-1-4169-6823-8
[1. Coming of age—Fiction. 2. Interpersonal relations—Fiction. 3. Beaches—Fiction. 4. Summer—Fiction. 5. Vacation homes—Fiction. 6. Friendship—Fiction.]
I. Title.
PZ7.H18944Su 2009
[Fic]—dc22
200802707

To all the important sister women in my life
and most especially Claire

Acknowledgments

First and always, thank you to the Pippin women:
Emily van Beek, Holly McGhee, and Samantha
Cosentino. Thank you to my editor extraordinaire
Emily Meehan, who supports me like no other, as well
as Courtney Bongiolatti, Lucy Ruth Cummins, and
everyone at S&S. Many thanks to Jenna and Beverly
and the Calhoun School for their continuous support
of my writing life. Thanks to my writing group the
Longstockings, and one Longstocking in particular,
who has sat across from me every Monday and cheered
me on—Siobhan, I'm looking at you. And thank you to
Aram, who inspired me to write about the forever kind
of friendship, the kind that spans over boyfriends and
beaches and children and lifetimes.

I say, "I can't believe you're really here."

He sounds almost shy when he says, "Me neither." And then he hesitates. "Are you still coming with me?"

I can't believe he even has to ask. I would go anywhere. "Yes," I tell him. It feels like nothing else exists outside of that word, this moment. There's just us. Everything that happened this past summer, and every summer before it, has all led up to this. To now.

chapter *one*

We'd been driving for about seven thousand years. Or at least that's how it felt. My brother, Steven, drove slower than our Granna. I sat next to him in the passenger seat with my feet up on the dashboard. Meanwhile, my mother was passed out in the backseat. Even when she slept, she looked alert, like at any second she could wake up and direct traffic.

"Go faster," I urged Steven, poking him in the shoulder. "Let's pass that kid on the bike."

Steven shrugged me off. "Never touch the driver," he said. "And take your dirty feet off my dashboard."

I wiggled my toes back and forth. They looked pretty clean to me. "It's not your dashboard. It's gonna be my car soon, you know."

"If you ever get your license," he scoffed. "People like you shouldn't even be allowed to drive."

"Hey, look," I said, pointing out the window. "That guy in a wheelchair just lapped us!"

Steven ignored me, and so I started to fiddle with the radio. One of my favorite things about going to the beach was the radio stations. I was as familiar with them as I was with the ones back home, and listening to Q94 made me just really know inside that I was there, at the beach.

I found my favorite station, the one that played everything from pop to oldies to hip-hop. Tom Petty was singing "Free Fallin'." I sang right along with him. "She's a good girl, crazy 'bout Elvis. Loves horses and her boyfriend too."

Steven reached over to switch stations, and I slapped his hand away. "Belly, your voice makes me want to run this car into the ocean." He pretended to swerve right.

I sang even louder, which woke up my mother, and she started to sing too. We both had terrible voices, and Steven shook his head in his disgusted Steven way. He hated being outnumbered. It was what bothered him most about our parents being divorced, being the lone guy, without our dad to take his side.

We drove through town slowly, and even though I'd just teased Steven about it, I didn't really mind. I loved this drive, this moment. Seeing the town again, Jimmy's Crab Shack, the Putt Putt, all the surf shops. It was like coming home after you'd been gone a long, long time. It held a million promises of summer and of what just might be.

As we got closer and closer to the house, I could feel that familiar flutter in my chest. We were almost there.

I rolled down the window and took it all in. The air tasted just the same, smelled just the same. The wind making my hair feel sticky, the salty sea breeze, all of it felt just right. Like it had been waiting for me to get there.

Steven elbowed me. "Are you thinking about Conrad?" he asked mockingly.

For once the answer was no. "No," I snapped.

My mother stuck her head in between our two seats. "Belly, do you still like Conrad? From the looks of things last summer, I thought there might be something between you and Jeremiah."

"WHAT? You and Jeremiah?" Steven looked sickened. "What happened with you and Jeremiah?"

"Nothing," I told them both. I could feel the flush rising up from my chest. I wished I had a tan already to cover it up. "Mom, just because two people are good friends, it doesn't mean there's anything going on. Please never bring that up again."

My mother leaned back into the backseat. "Done," she said. Her voice had that note of finality that I knew Steven wouldn't be able to break through.

Because he was Steven, he tried anyway. "What happened with you and Jeremiah? You can't say something like that and not explain."

"Get over it," I told him. Telling Steven anything

would only give him ammunition to make fun of me. And anyway, there was nothing to tell. There had never been anything to tell, not really.

Conrad and Jeremiah were Beck's boys. Beck was Susannah Fisher, formerly Susannah Beck. My mother was the only one who called her Beck. They'd known each other since they were nine—blood sisters, they called each other. And they had the scars to prove it—identical marks on their wrists that looked like hearts.

Susannah told me that when I was born, she knew I was destined for one of her boys. She said it was fate. My mother, who didn't normally go in for that kind of thing, said it would be perfect, as long as I'd had at least a few loves before I settled down. Actually, she said "lovers," but that word made me cringe. Susannah put her hands on my cheeks and said, "Belly, you have my unequivocal blessing. I'd hate to lose my boys to anyone else."

We'd been going to Susannah's beach house in Cousins Beach every summer since I was a baby, since before I was born even. For me, Cousins was less about the town and more about the house. The house was my world. We had our own stretch of beach, all to ourselves. The summer house was made up of lots of things. The wraparound porch we used to run around on, jugs of sun tea, the swimming pool at night—but the boys, the boys most of all.

I always wondered what the boys looked like in

December. I tried to picture them in cranberry-colored scarves and turtleneck sweaters, rosy-cheeked and standing beside a Christmas tree, but the image always seemed false. I did not know the winter Jeremiah or the winter Conrad, and I was jealous of everyone who did. I got flip-flops and sunburned noses and swim trunks and sand. But what about those New England girls who had snowball fights with them in the woods? The ones who snuggled up to them while they waited for the car to heat up, the ones they gave their coats to when it was chilly outside. Well, Jeremiah, maybe. Not Conrad. Conrad would never; it wasn't his style. Either way, it didn't seem fair.

I'd sit next to the radiator in history class and wonder what they were doing, if they were warming their feet along the bottom of a radiator somewhere too. Counting the days until summer again. For me, it was almost like winter didn't count. Summer was what mattered. My whole life was measured in summers. Like I don't really begin living until June, until I'm at that beach, in that house.

Conrad was the older one, by a year and a half. He was dark, dark, dark. Completely unattainable, unavailable. He had a smirky kind of mouth, and I always found myself staring at it. Smirky mouths make you want to kiss them, to smooth them out and kiss the smirkiness away. Or maybe not away . . . but you want to control it somehow. Make it yours. It was exactly what I wanted to do with Conrad. Make him mine.

Jeremiah, though—he was my friend. He was nice to me. He was the kind of boy who still hugged his mother, still wanted to hold her hand even when he was technically too old for it. He wasn't embarrassed either. Jeremiah Fisher was too busy having fun to ever be embarrassed.

I bet Jeremiah was more popular than Conrad at school. I bet the girls liked him better. I bet that if it weren't for football, Conrad wouldn't be some big deal. He would just be quiet, moody Conrad, not a football god. And I liked that. I liked that Conrad preferred to be alone, playing his guitar. Like he was above all the stupid high school stuff. I liked to think that if Conrad went to my school, he wouldn't play football, he'd be on the lit mag, and he'd notice someone like me.

When we finally pulled up to the house, Jeremiah and Conrad were sitting out on the front porch. I leaned over Steven and honked the horn twice, which in our summer language meant, *Come help with the bags, stat.*

Conrad was eighteen now. He'd just had a birthday. He was taller than last summer, if you can believe it. His hair was cut short around his ears and was as dark as ever. Unlike Jeremiah's, whose hair had gotten longer, so he looked a little shaggy but in a good way—like a 1970s tennis player. When he was younger, it was curly yellow, almost platinum in the summer. Jeremiah hated his curls. For a while, Conrad had him convinced that crusts made your hair curly, so Jeremiah had stopped eating sandwich crusts, and Conrad would polish them off. As Jeremiah got older, though, his hair was less and less curly and more wavy. I missed his curls. Susannah called him her little angel, and he used to look like one, with his rosy cheeks and yellow curls. He still had the rosy cheeks.

Jeremiah made a megaphone with his hands and yelled, "Steve-o!"

I sat in the car and watched Steven amble up to them and hug the way guys do. The air smelled salty and wet, like it might rain seawater any second. I pretended to be tying the laces on my sneakers, but really I just wanted a moment to look at them, at the house for a little while, in private. The house was large and gray and white, and it looked like most every other house on the road, but better. It looked just the way I thought a beach house should look. It looked like home.

My mother got out of the car then too. "Hey, boys. Where's your mother?" she called out.

"Hey, Laurel. She's taking a nap," Jeremiah called back. Usually she came flying out of the house the second our car pulled up.

My mother walked over to them in about three strides, and she hugged them both, tightly. My mother's hug was as firm and solid as her handshake. She disappeared into the house with her sunglasses perched on the top of her head.

I got out of the car and slung my bag over my shoulder. They didn't even notice me walk up at first. But then they did. They really did. Conrad gave me a quick glance-over the way boys do at the mall. He had never looked at me like that before in my whole life. Not once. I could feel my flush from the car return. Jeremiah, on the other hand, did a double take. He looked at me like he didn't even recognize me. All of this happened in the span of about three seconds, but it felt much, much longer.

Conrad hugged me first, but a faraway kind of hug, careful not to get too close. He'd just gotten a haircut, and the skin around the nape of his neck looked pink and new, like a baby's. He smelled like the ocean. He smelled like Conrad. "I liked you better with glasses," he said, his lips close to my ear.

That stung. I shoved him away and said, "Well, too bad. My contacts are here to stay."

He smiled at me, and that smile—he just gets in. His smile did it every time. "I think you got a few new ones," he said, tapping me on the nose. He knew how self-conscious I was about my freckles and he still teased me every time.

Then Jeremiah grabbed me next, and he almost lifted me into the air. "Belly Button's all growed up," he crowed.

I laughed. "Put me down," I told him. "You smell like BO."

Jeremiah laughed loudly. "Same old Belly," he said, but he was staring at me like he wasn't quite sure who I was.

He cocked his head and said, "Something looks different about you, Belly."

I braced myself for the punch line. "What? I got contacts." I wasn't completely used to myself without glasses either. My best friend Taylor had been trying to convince me to get contacts since the sixth grade, and I'd finally listened.

He smiled. "It's not that. You just look different."

I went back to the car then, and the boys followed me. We unloaded the car quickly, and as soon as we were done, I picked up my suitcase and my book bag and headed straight for my old bedroom. My room was Susannah's from when she was a child. It had faded calico wallpaper and a white bedroom set. There was a music box I loved. When you opened it, there was a twirling ballerina that danced to the theme song from *Romeo and Juliet*, the old-timey version. I kept my jewelry in it. Everything about my room was old and faded, but I loved that about it. It felt like there might be secrets in the walls, in the four-poster bed, especially in that music box.

Seeing Conrad again, having him look at me that way, I felt like I needed a second to breathe. I grabbed the stuffed polar bear on my dresser and hugged him close to my chest—his name was Junior Mint, Junior for short. I sat down with Junior on my twin bed. My heart was beating so loudly I could hear it. Everything was the same but not. They had looked at me like I was a real girl, not just somebody's little sister.

chapter *two*

AGE 12

The first time I ever had my heart broken was at this house. I was twelve.

It was one of those really rare nights when the boys weren't all together—Steven and Jeremiah went on an overnight fishing trip with some boys they'd met at the arcade. Conrad said he didn't feel like going, and of course I wasn't invited, so it was just me and him.

Well, not together, but in the same house.

I was reading a romance novel in my room with my feet on the wall when Conrad walked by. He stopped and said, "Belly, what are you doing tonight?"

I folded the cover of my book over quickly. "Nothing," I said. I tried to keep my voice even, not too excited or eager. I had left my door open on purpose, hoping he'd stop by.

"Want to go to the boardwalk with me?" he asked. He sounded casual, almost too casual.

This was the moment I had been waiting for. This was it. I was finally old enough. Some part of me knew it too, it was ready. I glanced over at him, just as casual as he'd been. "Maybe. I have been craving a caramel apple."

"I'll buy one for you," he offered. "Just hurry up and put some clothes on and we'll go. Our moms are going to the movies; they'll drop us off on the way."

I sat up and said, "Okay."

As soon as Conrad left, I closed my door and ran over to my mirror. I took my hair out of its braids and brushed it. It was long that summer, almost to my waist. Then I changed out of my bathing suit and put on white shorts and my favorite gray shirt. My dad said it matched my eyes. I smeared some strawberry frosting lip gloss on my lips and tucked the tube into my pocket, for later. In case I needed to reapply.

In the car Susannah kept smiling at me in the rearview mirror. I gave her a look like, *Quit, please*—but I wanted to smile back. Conrad wasn't paying attention anyway. He was looking out the window the whole ride there.

"Have fun, kids," said Susannah, winking at me as I closed my door.

Conrad bought me a caramel apple first. He bought himself a soda, but that was it—usually he ate at least an apple or two, or a funnel cake. He seemed nervous, which made me feel less nervous.

As we walked down the boardwalk, I let my arm hang loose—*in case*. But he didn't reach for it. It was one of those perfect summer nights, the kind where there's a cool breeze and not one drop of rain. There would be rain tomorrow, but that night there were cool breezes and that was it.

I said, "Let's sit down so I can eat my apple," so we did. We sat on a bench that faced the beach.

I bit into my apple, carefully; I was worried I might get caramel all stuck in my teeth, and then how would he kiss me?

He sipped his Coke noisily, and then glanced down at his watch. "When you finish that, let's go to the ring-toss."

He wanted to win me a stuffed animal! I already knew which one I'd pick too—the polar bear with wire-frame glasses and a scarf. I'd had my eye on it all summer. I could already picture myself showing it off to Taylor. Oh, that? Conrad Fisher won it for me.

I wolfed down the rest of my apple in about two bites. "'Kay," I said, wiping my mouth with the back of my hand. "Let's go."

Conrad walked straight over to the ringtoss, and I had to walk superquick to keep up. As usual, he wasn't talking much, so I talked even more to make up for it. "I think when we get back, my mom might finally get cable. Steven and my dad and I have been trying to convince her for forever. She claims to be so against TV, but then she watches movies on A&E, like, the whole time we're here. It's so hypocritical," I said, and my voice trailed off when I saw that Conrad wasn't even listening. He was watching the girl who worked the ringtoss.

She looked about fourteen or fifteen. The first thing I noticed about her was her shorts. They were canary yellow, and they were really, really short. The exact same kind of shorts that the boys had made fun of me for wearing two days before. I felt so good about buying those shorts with Susannah, and then the boys had laughed at me for it. The shorts looked a whole lot better on her.

Her legs were skinny and freckled, and so were her arms. Everything about her was skinny, even her lips. Her hair was long and wavy. It was red, but it was so light it was almost peach. I think it might have been the prettiest hair I'd ever seen. She had it pulled over to the side, and it was so long that she had to keep flicking it away as she handed people rings.

Conrad had come to the boardwalk for her. He'd brought me because he hadn't wanted to come alone and he hadn't wanted Steven and Jeremiah to give him a hard time. That was it. That was the whole reason. I could see it all in the way he looked at her, the way he almost seemed to hold his breath.

"Do you know her?" I asked.

He looked startled, like he'd forgotten I was there. "Her? No, not really."

I bit my lip. "Well, do you want to?"

"Do I want to what?" Conrad was confused, which was annoying.

"Do you want to know her?" I asked impatiently.

"I guess."

I grabbed him by his shirt sleeve and walked right up to the booth. The girl smiled at us, and I smiled back, but it was just for show. I was playing a part. "How many rings?" she asked. She had braces, but on her they looked interesting, like teeth jewelry and not like orthodontics.

"We'll take three," I told her. "I like your shorts."

"Thanks," she said.

Conrad cleared his throat. "They're nice."

"I thought you said they were too short when I wore the exact same pair two days ago." I turned to the girl and said, "Conrad is so overprotective. Do you have a big brother?"

She laughed. "No." To Conrad she said, "You think they're too short?"

He blushed. I'd never seen him blush before, not in the whole time I'd known him. I had a feeling it might be the last time. I made a big show of looking at my watch and said, "Con, I'm gonna go ride the Ferris wheel before we leave. Win me a prize, okay?"

Conrad nodded quickly, and I said bye to the girl and

left. I walked over to the Ferris wheel as fast as I could so they wouldn't see me cry.

Later on, I found out the girl's name was Angie. Conrad ended up winning me the polar bear with the wire-frame glasses and scarf. He said Angie told him it was the best prize they had. He said he thought I'd like it too. I told him I'd rather have had the giraffe, but thanks anyway. I named him Junior Mint, and I left him where he belonged, at the summer house.

chapter *three*

After I unpacked, I went straight down to the pool, where I knew the boys would be. They were lying around on the deck chairs, their dirty bare feet hanging off the edges.

As soon as Jeremiah saw me, he sprang up. "Ladies and Gentlemen-men-men," he began dramatically, bowing like a circus ringmaster. "I do believe it is time . . . for our first belly flop of the summer."

I inched away from them uneasily. Too fast a movement, and it would be all over—they'd chase me then. "No way," I said.

Then Conrad and Steven stood up, circling me. "You can't fight tradition," Steven said. Conrad just grinned evilly.

"I'm too old for this," I said desperately. I walked

backward, and that's when they grabbed me. Steven and Jeremiah each took a wrist.

"Come on, guys," I said, trying to wriggle out of their grasp. I dragged my feet, but they pulled me along. I knew it was futile to resist, but I always tried, even though the bottoms of my feet got burned along the pavement in the process.

"Ready?" Jeremiah said, lifting me up under my armpits.

Conrad grabbed my feet, and then Steven took my right arm while Jeremiah hung on to my left. They swung me back and forth like I was a sack of flour. "I hate you guys," I yelled over their laughter.

"One," Jeremiah began.

"Two," Steven said.

"And three," Conrad finished. Then they launched me into the pool, clothes and all. I hit the water with a loud smack. Underwater, I could hear them busting up.

The Belly Flop was something they'd started about a million summers ago. Probably it had been Steven. I hated it. Even though it was one of the only times I was included in their fun, I hated being the brunt of it. It made me feel utterly powerless, and it was a reminder that I was an outsider, too weak to fight them, all because I was a girl. Somebody's little sister.

I used to cry about it, run to Susannah and my mother, but it didn't do any good. The boys just accused me of being a tattletale. Not this time, though. This time I was going to be a good sport. If I was a good sport, maybe that would take away some of their joy.

When I came up to the surface, I smiled and said, "You guys are ten-year-olds."

"For life," Steven said smugly. His smuggy face made me want to splash him and soak him and his precious Hugo Boss sunglasses that he worked for three weeks to pay for.

Then I said, "I think you twisted my ankle, Conrad." I pretended to have trouble swimming over to them.

He walked over to the edge of the pool. "I'm pretty sure you'll live," he said, smirking.

"At least help me out," I demanded.

He squatted and gave me his hand, which I took.

"Thanks," I said giddily. Then I gripped tight and pulled his arm as hard as I could. He stumbled, fell forward, and landed in the pool with a splash even bigger than mine. I think I laughed harder right then than I've laughed in my whole life. So did Jeremiah and Steven. I think maybe all of Cousins Beach heard us laughing.

Conrad's head bobbed up quickly, and he swam over to me in about two strokes. I worried he might be mad, but he wasn't, not completely. He was smiling but in a threatening kind of way. I dodged away from him. "Can't catch me," I said gleefully. "Too slow!"

Every time he came close, I swam away. "Marco," I called out, giggling.

Jeremiah and Steven, who were headed back to the house, said, "Polo!"

Which made me laugh, which made me slow to swim away, and Conrad caught my foot. "Let go," I gasped, still laughing.

Conrad shook his head. "I thought I was too slow," he said, treading water closer to me. We were in the diving well. His white T-shirt was soaked through, and I could see the pinky gold of his skin.

There was this weird stillness between us all of a sudden. He still held on to my foot, and I was trying to stay afloat. For a second I wished Jeremiah and Steven were still there. I didn't know why.

"Let go," I said again.

He pulled on my foot, drawing me closer. Being this close to him was making me feel dizzy and nervous. I said it again, one last time, even though I didn't mean it. "Conrad, let go of me."

He did. And then he dunked me. It didn't matter. I was already holding my breath.

chapter *four*

Susannah came down from her nap a little while after we put on dry clothes, apologizing for missing our big homecoming. She still looked sleepy and her hair was all feathery on one side like a kid's. She and my mother hugged first, fierce and long. My mother looked so happy to see her that she was teary, and my mother was never teary.

Then it was my turn. Susannah swept me in for a hug, the close kind that's long enough to make you wonder how long it's going to last, who'll pull away first.

"You look thin," I told her, partly because it was true and partly because I knew she loved to hear it. She was always on a diet, always watching what she ate. To me, she was perfect.

"Thanks, honey," Susannah said, finally letting me go,

looking at me from arm's length. She shook her head and said, "When did you go and grow up? When did you turn into this phenomenal woman?"

I smiled self-consciously, glad that the boys were upstairs and not around to hear this. "I look pretty much the same."

"You've always been lovely, but oh honey, look at you." She shook her head like she was in awe of me. "You're so pretty. So pretty. You're going to have an amazing, amazing summer. It'll be a summer you'll never forget." Susannah always spoke in absolutes like that—and when she did, it sounded like a proclamation, like it would come true because she said so.

The thing is, Susannah was right. It was a summer I'd never, ever forget. It was the summer everything began. It was the summer I turned pretty. Because for the first time, I felt it. Pretty, I mean. Every summer up to this one, I believed it'd be different. Life would be different. And that summer, it finally was. I was.

chapter *five*

Dinner the first night was always the same: a big pot of spicy bouillabaisse that Susannah cooked up while she waited for us to arrive. Lots of shrimp and crab legs and squid—she knew I loved squid. Even when I was little, I would pick out the squid and save it for last. Susannah put the pot in the middle of the table, along with a few crusty loaves of French bread from the bakery nearby. Each of us would get a bowl, and we'd help ourselves to the pot all throughout dinner, dipping the ladle back into the pot. Susannah and my mother always had red wine, and us kids had grape Fanta, but on that night there were wineglasses for everyone.

"I think we're all old enough to partake now, don't you, Laur?" Susannah said as we sat down.

"I don't know about that," my mother began, but then

she stopped. "Oh, all right. Fine. I'm being provincial, isn't that right, Beck?"

Susannah laughed and uncorked the bottle. "You? Never," she said, pouring a little wine for each of us. "It's a special night. It's the first night of summer."

Conrad drank his wine in about two gulps. He drank it like he was used to drinking it. I guess a lot can happen over the course of a year. He said, "It's not the first night of summer, Mom."

"Oh, yes it is. Summer doesn't start until our friends get here," Susannah said, reaching across the table and touching my hand, and Conrad's, too.

He jerked away from her, almost by accident. Susannah didn't seem to notice, but I did. I always noticed Conrad.

Jeremiah must have seen it too, because he changed the subject. "Belly, check out my latest scar," he said, pulling up his shirt. "I scored three field goals that night." Jeremiah played football. He was proud of all of his battle scars.

I leaned in next to him to get a good look. It was a long scar that was just beginning to fade, right across the bottom of his stomach. Clearly, he'd been working out. His stomach was flat and hard, and it hadn't looked like that last summer even. He looked bigger than Conrad now. "Wow," I said.

Conrad snorted. "Jere just wants to show off his two-pack," he said, breaking off a piece of bread and dipping it into his bowl. "Why don't you show all of us, and not just Belly?"

"Yeah, show us, Jere," Steven said, grinning.

Jeremiah grinned right back. To Conrad he said, "You're just jealous because you quit." Conrad had quit football? That was news to me.

"Conrad, you quit, man?" Steven asked. I guessed it was news to him, too. Conrad was really good; Susannah used to mail us his newspaper clippings. He and Jeremiah had been on the team together these last two years, but it was Conrad who'd been the star.

Conrad shrugged indifferently. His hair was still wet from the pool, and so was mine. "It got boring," he said.

"What he means is, he got boring," Jeremiah said. Then he stood up and pulled off his shirt. "Pretty nice, huh?"

Susannah threw her head back and laughed, and my mother did too. "Sit down, Jeremiah," she said, shaking the loaf of bread at him like a sword.

"What do you think, Belly?" he asked me. He looked like he was winking even though he wasn't.

"Pretty nice," I agreed, trying not to smile.

"Now it's Belly's turn to show off," Conrad said mockingly.

"Belly doesn't need to show off. We can all see how lovely she is just looking at her," Susannah said, sipping her wine and smiling at me.

"Lovely? Yeah, right," said Steven. "She's a lovely pain in my ass."

"Steven," my mother warned.

"What? What'd I say?" he asked.

"Steven's too much of a pig to understand the concept of lovely," I said sweetly. I pushed the bread to him. "Oink, oink, Steven. Have some more bread."

"Don't mind if I do," he said, breaking off a crusty chunk.

"Belly, tell us about all the hot friends you're gonna set me up with," Jeremiah said.

"Didn't we already try that once?" I said. "Don't tell me you've forgotten about Taylor Jewel already."

Everyone busted up laughing then, even Conrad.

Jeremiah's cheeks turned pink, but he was laughing too, and shaking his head. "You're not a nice girl, Belly," he said. "There's plenty of cute girls at the country club, so don't worry about me. Worry about Con. He's the one missing out."

The original plan was for both Jeremiah and Conrad to work at the country club as lifeguards. Conrad had done it the summer before. This summer Jeremiah was old enough to do it with him, but Conrad changed his mind at the last minute and decided to bus tables at the fancy seafood buffet instead.

We used to go there all the time. Kids twelve and younger could eat there for twenty dollars. There was a time when I was the only one twelve or younger. My mother always made sure to tell the waiter that I was younger than twelve. As, like, principle. Every time she did it, I felt like disappearing. I wished I was invisible. It wasn't that the boys even made a big deal out of it, which they easily could have, but it was the feeling different, like an outsider, that I hated. I hated it being pointed out. I just wanted to be like them.

chapter *six*
AGE 10

Right off the bat, the boys were a unit. Conrad was the leader. His word was pretty much law. Steven was his second in command, and Jeremiah was the jester. That first night, Conrad decided that the boys were going to sleep on the beach in sleeping bags and make a fire. He was a Boy Scout; he knew all about that kind of stuff.

Jealously, I watched them plan. Especially when they packed the graham crackers and marshmallows. Don't take the whole box, I wanted to tell them. I didn't, though—it wasn't my place. It wasn't even my house.

"Steven, make sure you bring the flashlight," Conrad directed. Steven nodded quickly. I had never seen him follow orders before. He looked up to Conrad, who was eight months older; it had always been that way.

Everybody had somebody but me. I wished I was at home, making butterscotch sundaes with my dad and eating them on our living room floor.

"Jeremiah, don't forget the cards," Conrad added, rolling up a sleeping bag.

Jeremiah saluted him and danced a little jig, which made me giggle. "Sir, yes, sir." He turned to me on the couch and said, "Conrad is bossy like our dad. Don't feel like you have to listen to him or anything."

Jeremiah talking to me made me feel brave enough to say, "Can I come too?"

Right away Steven said, "No. Guys only. Right, Con?"

Conrad hesitated. "Sorry, Belly," he said, and he really did look sorry for a second. Two seconds, even. Then he went back to rolling his sleeping bag.

I turned away from them and faced the TV. "That's okay. I don't really care anyway."

"Ooh, watch out, Belly's gonna cry," Steven said joyously. To Jeremiah and Conrad he said, "When she doesn't get her way, she cries. Our dad always falls for it."

"Shut up, Steven!" I yelled. I was worried I really might cry. The last thing I needed was to be a crybaby our first night. Then they'd never take me along for real.

"Belly's gonna cry," Steven said in a singsong voice. Then he and Jeremiah started to dance a jig together.

"Leave her alone," Conrad said.

Steven stopped dancing. "What?" he said, confused.

"You guys are so immature," Conrad said, shaking his head.

I watched them pick up their gear and get ready to leave. I was about to lose my chance to camp, to be a part of the gang. Quickly I said, "Steven, if you don't let me go, I'll tell Mom."

Steven's face twisted. "No, you won't. Mom hates it when you tattletale."

It was true, my mother hated it when I told on Steven for things like this. She'd say he needed his own time, that I could go the next time around, that it would be more fun at the house with her and Beck anyway. I sank into the couch, arms crossed. I'd lost my chance. Now I just looked like a tattletale, a baby.

On the way out Jeremiah turned around and danced a quick jig for me, and I couldn't help it, I laughed. Over his shoulder Conrad said, "Good night, Belly."

And that was it. I was in love.

chapter *seven*

I didn't notice right away that their family had more money than ours. The beach house wasn't some fancy kind of place. It was a real honest-to-God beach house, the kind that's lived in and comfortable. It had faded old seersucker couches and a creaking La-Z-Boy us kids always fought over, and peeling white paint and hardwood floors that had been bleached by the sun.

But it was a big house, room enough for all of us and more. They'd built an addition years ago. On one end there was my mother's room, Susannah and Mr. Fisher's room, and an empty guest room. On the other end was my room, another guest room, and the room the boys shared, which I was jealous of. There used to be bunk beds and a twin in that room, and I hated that I had to sleep all alone in mine when I could hear them giggling and whispering all night through the wall. A couple of times the boys let me sleep in there too, but only when they had some especially gruesome story they wanted to tell. I was a good audience. I always screamed at all the right places.

Since we've gotten older, the boys have stopped sharing a room. Steven started staying over on the parents' end, and Jeremiah and Conrad both had their rooms on my end. The boys and I have shared a bathroom since the beginning. Ours is on our end of the house, and then my mother has her own, and Susannah's is connected to the master bedroom. There are two sinks—Jeremiah and Conrad shared one, and Steven and I shared the other.

When we were little, the boys never put the seat down, and they still didn't. It was a constant reminder that I was different, that I wasn't one of them. Little things have changed, though. It used to be that they left water all over the place, either from splash fights or from just being careless. Now that they shaved, they left their little chin hairs all over the sink. The counter was crowded with their different deodorants and shaving cream and cologne.

They had more cologne than I had perfume—one pink French bottle my dad bought me for Christmas when I was thirteen. It smelled like vanilla and burnt sugar and lemon. I think his grad student girlfriend picked it out. He wasn't good at that sort of thing. Anyway, I didn't leave my perfume in the bathroom mixed in with all their stuff. I kept it on the dresser in my room, and I never wore it anyway. I didn't know why I even brought it with me.

chapter *eight*

After dinner I stayed downstairs on the couch and so did Conrad. He sat there across from me, strumming chords on his guitar with his head bent.

"So I heard you have a girlfriend," I said. "I heard it's pretty serious."

"My brother has a big mouth." About a month before we'd left for Cousins, Jeremiah had called Steven. They were on the phone for a while, and I hid outside Steven's bedroom door listening. Steven didn't say a whole lot on his end, but it seemed like a serious conversation. I burst into his room and asked him what they were talking about, and Steven accused me of being a nosy little spy, and then he finally told me that Conrad had a girlfriend.

"So what's she like?" I didn't look at him when I said

this. I was afraid he'd be able to see how much I cared.

Conrad cleared his throat. "We broke up," he said.

I almost gasped. My heart did a little ping. "Your mom is right, you are a heartbreaker." I meant it to come out as a joke, but the words rang in my head and in the air like some kind of declaration.

He flinched. "She dumped me," he said <u>flatly</u>.

I couldn't imagine anyone breaking up with Conrad. I wondered what she was like. Suddenly she was this <u>compelling</u>, actual person in my mind. "What was her name?"

"What does it matter?" he said, his voice rough. Then, "Aubrey. Her name is Aubrey."

"Why did she break up with you?" I couldn't help myself. I was too curious. Who was this girl? I pictured someone with pale white blond hair and turquoise eyes, someone with perfect cuticles and oval-shaped nails. I'd always had to keep mine short for piano, and then after I quit, I still kept them short, because I was used to them that way.

Conrad put down the guitar and stared off into space moodily. "She said I changed."

"And did you?"

"I don't know. Everybody changes. You did."

"How did I change?"

He shrugged and picked up his guitar again. "Like I said, everybody changes."

Conrad started playing the guitar in middle school. I hated it when he played the guitar. He'd sit there, strumming, halfway paying attention, only halfway present. He'd hum to himself, and he was someplace else. We'd be watching TV, or playing cards, and he'd be strumming the guitar. Or he'd be in his room, practicing. For what, I didn't know. All I knew was that it took time away from us.

"Listen to this," he'd said once, stretching out his headphones so I had one and he had the other. Our heads touched. "Isn't it amazing?"

"It" was Pearl Jam. Conrad was as happy and enthralled as if he had discovered them himself. I'd never heard of them, but at that moment, it was the best song I'd ever heard. I went out and bought *Ten* and listened to it on repeat. When I listened to track five, "Black," it was like I was there, in that moment all over again.

After the summer was over, when I got back home, I went to the music store and bought the sheet music and learned to play it on the piano. I thought one day I could accompany Conrad and we could be, like, a band. Which was so stupid, the summer house didn't even have a piano. Susannah tried to get one for the summer house, so I could practice, but my mother wouldn't let her.

chapter *nine*

At night when I couldn't sleep, I'd sneak downstairs and go for a swim in the pool. I'd start doing laps, and I'd keep going until I felt tired. When I went to bed, my muscles felt nice and sore but also shivery and relaxed. I loved bundling myself up after a swim in one of Susannah's cornflower blue bath sheets—I'd never even heard of bath sheets before Susannah. And then, tiptoeing back upstairs, falling asleep with my hair still wet. You sleep so well after you've been in the water. It's like no other feeling.

Two summers ago Susannah found me down there, and some nights she'd swim with me. I'd be underwater, doing my laps, and I'd feel her dive in and start to swim on the other side of the pool. We wouldn't talk; we'd just swim, but it was comforting to have her there. It was the only time that summer that I ever saw her without her wig.

Back then, because of the chemo, Susannah wore her wig all the time. No one saw her without it, not even my mother. Susannah had had the prettiest hair. Long, caramel-colored, soft as cotton candy. Her wig didn't even compare, and it was real human hair and everything, the best money could buy. After the chemo, after her hair grew back, she kept it short, cut right below her chin. It was pretty, but it wasn't the same. Looking at her now, you'd never know who she used to be, with her hair long like a teenager, like mine.

That first night of the summer, I couldn't sleep. It always took me a night or two to get used to my bed again, even though I'd slept in it pretty much every summer of my life. I tossed and turned for a while, and then I couldn't stand it anymore. I put on my bathing suit, my old swim team one that barely fit anymore, with the gold stripes and the racerback. It was my first night swim of the summer.

When I swam alone at night, everything felt so much clearer. Listening to myself breathe in and out, it made me feel calm and steady and strong. Like I could swim forever.

I swam back and forth a few times, and on the fourth lap, I started to flip turn, but I kicked something solid. I came up for air and saw it was Conrad's leg. He was sitting on the edge of the pool with his feet dangling in.

He'd been watching me that whole time. And he was smoking a cigarette.

I stayed underwater up to my chin—I was suddenly aware of how my bathing suit was too small for me now. There was no way I was getting out of the water with him still there.

"Since when did you start smoking?" I asked accusingly. "And what are you doing down here anyway?"

"Which do you want me to answer first?" He had that amused, condescending Conrad look on his face, the one that drove me crazy.

I swam over to the wall and rested my arms on the edge. "The second."

"I couldn't sleep so I went for a walk," he said, shrugging. He was lying. He'd only come outside to smoke.

"How did you know I was out here?" I demanded.

"You always swim out here at night, Belly. Come on." He took a drag of his cigarette.

He knew I swam at night? I'd thought it was my special secret, mine and Susannah's. I wondered how long he had known. I wondered if everyone knew. I didn't even know why it mattered, but it did. To me, it did. "Okay, fine. Then when did you start smoking?"

"I don't know. Last year, maybe." He was being vague on purpose. It was maddening.

"Well, you shouldn't. You should quit right now. Are you addicted?"

He laughed. "No."

"Then quit. If you put your mind to it, I know you can." If he put his mind to it, I knew he could do anything.

"Maybe I don't want to."

"You should, Conrad. Smoking is so bad for you."

"What will you give me if I do?" he asked teasingly. He held the cigarette in the air, above his beer can.

The air felt different all of a sudden. It felt charged, electric, like I had been zapped by a thunderbolt. I let go of the edge and started to tread water, away from him. It felt like forever before I spoke. "Nothing," I said. "You should quit for yourself."

"You're right," he said, and the moment was over. He stood up and ground his cigarette out on the top of the can. "Good night, Belly. Don't stay out here too late. You never know what kind of monsters come out at night."

Everything felt normal again. I splashed water at his legs as he walked away. "Screw you," I said to his back. A long time ago Conrad and Jeremiah and Steven convinced me that there was a child killer on the loose, the kind who liked chubby little girls with brown hair and grayish-blue eyes.

"Wait! Are you quitting or not?" I yelled.

He didn't answer me. He just laughed. I could tell by the way his shoulders shook as he closed the gate.

After he left, I fell back into the water and floated. I

could feel my heart beating through my ears. It thudded quick-quick-quick like a metronome. Conrad was different. I'd sensed something even at dinner, before he'd told me about Aubrey. He had changed. And yet, the way he affected me was still the same. It felt just exactly the same. It felt like I was at the top of the Grizzly at Kings Dominion, right about to go down the first hill.

chapter *ten*

"Belly, have you called your dad yet?" my mother asked me.

"No."

"I think you should call him and tell him how you're doing."

I rolled my eyes. "I doubt he's sitting at home worrying about it."

"Still."

"Well, have you made Steven call him?" I countered.

"No, I haven't," she said, her tone level. "Your dad and Steven are about to spend two weeks together looking at colleges. You, on the other hand, won't get to see him until the end of summer."

Why did she have to be so reasonable? Everything was that way with her. My mother was the only person I knew who could have a reasonable divorce.

My mother got up and handed me the phone. "Call your father," she said, leaving the room. She always left the room when I called my father, like she was giving me privacy. As if there were some secrets I needed to tell my father that I couldn't tell him in front of her.

I didn't call him. I put the phone back in its cradle. He should be the one calling me; not the other way around. He was the father; I was just the kid. And anyway, dads didn't belong in the summer house. Not my father and not Mr. Fisher. Sure, they'd come to visit, but it wasn't their place. They didn't belong to it. Not the way we all did, the mothers and us kids.

chapter *eleven*
AGE 9

We were playing cards outside on the porch, and my mother and Susannah were drinking margaritas and playing their own card game. The sun was starting to go down, and soon the mothers would have to go inside and boil corn and hot dogs. But not yet. First they played cards.

"Laurel, why do you call my mom Beck when everyone else calls her Susannah?" Jeremiah wanted to know. He and my brother, Steven, were a team, and they were losing. Card games bored Jeremiah, and he was always looking for something more interesting to do, to talk about.

"Because her maiden name is Beck," my mother explained, grinding out a cigarette. They only smoked when they were together, so it was a special occasion. My mother said smoking with Susannah made her feel young again. I said it would shorten her life span by years but she waved off my worries and called me a doomsdayer.

"What's a maiden name?" Jeremiah asked. My brother tapped Jeremiah's hand of cards to get him back into the game, but Jeremiah ignored him.

"It's a lady's name before she gets married, dipwad," said Conrad.

"Don't call him dipwad, Conrad," Susannah said automatically, sorting through her hand.

"But why does she have to change her name at all?" Jeremiah wondered.

"She doesn't. I didn't. My name is Laurel Dunne, same as the day I was born. Nice, huh?" My mother liked to feel superior to Susannah for not changing her name. "After all, why should a woman have to change her name for a man? She shouldn't."

"Laurel, please shut up," said Susannah, throwing a few cards down onto the table. "Gin."

My mother sighed, and threw her cards down too. "I don't want to play gin anymore. Let's play something else. Let's play go fish with these guys."

"Sore loser," Susannah said.

"Mom, we're not playing go fish. We're playing hearts, and you can't play because you always try to cheat," I said. Conrad was my partner, and I was pretty sure we were going to win. I had picked him on purpose. Conrad was good at winning. He was the fastest swimmer, the best boogie boarder, and he always, always won at cards.

Susannah clapped her hands together and laughed. "Laur, this girl is you all over again."

My mother said, "No, Belly's her father's daughter," and they exchanged this secret look that made me want to say, "What, what?" But I knew my mother would never say. She was a secret-keeper, always had been. And I guessed I did look like my father: I had his eyes that turned up at the corners, a little girl version of his nose, his chin that jutted out. All I had of my mother was her hands.

Then the moment was over and Susannah smiled at me and said, "You're absolutely right, Belly. Your mother does cheat. She's always cheated at hearts. Cheaters never prosper, children."

Susannah was always calling us children, but the thing was, I didn't even mind. Normally I would. But the way Susannah said it, it didn't seem like a bad thing, not like we were small and babyish. Instead it sounded like we had our whole lives in front of us.

chapter *twelve*

Mr. Fisher would pop in throughout the summer, an occasional weekend and always the first week of August. He was a banker, and getting away for any real length of time was, according to him, simply impossible. And anyway, it was better without him there, when it was just us. When Mr. Fisher came to town, which wasn't very often, I stood up a little straighter. Everyone did. Well, except Susannah and my mother, of course. The funny thing was, my mother had known Mr. Fisher for as long as Susannah had—the three of them had gone to college together, and their school was small.

Susannah always told me to call Mr. Fisher "Adam," but I could never do it. It just didn't sound right. Mr. Fisher was what sounded right, so that's what I called him, and that's what Steven called him too. I think something about him inspired people to call him that, and not just kids, either. I think he preferred it that way.

He'd arrive at dinnertime on Friday night, and we'd wait for him. Susannah would fix his favorite drink and have it ready, ginger and Maker's Mark. My mother teased her for waiting on him, but Susannah didn't mind. My mother teased Mr. Fisher, too, in fact. He teased her right back. Maybe teasing isn't the right word. It was more like bickering. They bickered a lot, but they smiled, too. It was funny: My mother and father had rarely argued, but they hadn't smiled that much either.

I guess Mr. Fisher was good-looking, for a dad. He was better-looking than my father anyway, but he was also vainer than him. I don't know that he was as good-looking as Susannah was beautiful, but that might've just been because I loved Susannah more than almost anyone, and who could ever measure up to a person like that? Sometimes it's like people are a million times more beautiful to you in your mind. It's like you see them through a special lens—but maybe if it's how you see them, that's how they really are. It's like the whole tree falling in the forest thing.

Mr. Fisher gave us kids a twenty anytime we went anywhere. Conrad was always in charge of it. "For ice cream," he'd say. "Buy yourselves something sweet." Something sweet. It was always something sweet. Conrad worshipped him. His dad was his hero. For a long time, anyway. Longer than most people. I think my dad stopped being my hero when I saw him with one of his PhD students after he and my mother separated. She wasn't even pretty.

It would be easy to blame my dad for the whole thing—the divorce, the new apartment. But if I blamed anyone, it was my mother. Why did she have to be so calm, so placid? At least my father cried. At least he was in pain. My mother said nothing, revealed nothing. Our family broke up, and she just went on. It wasn't right.

When we got home from the beach that summer, my dad had already moved out—his first-edition Hemingways, his chess set, his Billy Joel CDs, Claude. Claude was his cat, and he belonged to my dad in a way that he didn't to anyone else. It was only right that he took Claude. Still, I was sad. In a way, Claude being gone was almost worse than my dad, because Claude was so permanent in the way he lived in our house, the way he inhabited every single space. It was like he owned the place.

My dad took me out for lunch to Applebee's, and he said, apologetically, "I'm sorry I took Claude. Do you miss him?" He had Russian dressing on his beard, newly grown out, for most of the lunch. It was annoying. The beard was annoying; the lunch was annoying.

"No," I said. I couldn't look up from my French onion soup. "He's yours anyway."

So my father got Claude, and my mother got Steven and me. It worked out for everyone. We saw my father most weekends. We'd stay at his new apartment that smelled like mildew, no matter how much <u>incense</u> he lit.

I hated incense, and so did my mother. It made me sneeze. I think it made my father feel independent and exotic to light all the incense he wanted, in his new pad, as he called it. As soon as I walked into the apartment, I said accusingly, "Have you been lighting incense in here?" Had he forgotten about my allergy already?

Guiltily, my father admitted that yes, he had lit some incense, but he wouldn't do it anymore. He still did, though. He did it when I wasn't there, out the window, but I could still smell the stuff.

It was a two-bedroom apartment; he slept in the master bedroom, and I slept in the other one in a little twin bed with pink sheets. My brother slept on the pullout couch. Which, I was actually jealous of, because he got to stay up watching TV. All my room had was a bed and a white dresser set that I barely even used. Only one drawer had clothes in it. The rest were empty. There was a bookshelf too, with books my father had bought for me. My father was always buying me books. He kept hoping I'd turn out smart like him, someone who loved words, loved to read. I did like to read, but not the way he wanted me to. Not in the way of being, like, a scholar. I liked novels, not nonfiction. And I hated those scratchy pink sheets. If he had asked me, I would have told him yellow, not pink.

He did try, though. In his own way, he tried. He bought a secondhand piano and crammed it into the dining room, just for me. So I could still practice even when I stayed over there, he said. I hardly did, though— the piano was out of tune, and I never had the heart to tell him.

It's part of why I longed for summer. It meant I didn't have to stay at my father's sad little apartment. It wasn't that I didn't like seeing him: I did. I missed him so much. But that apartment, it was depressing. I wished I could see him at our house. Our real house. I wished it could be like it used to be. And since my mother had us most of the summer, he took Steven and me on a trip when we got back. Usually it was to Florida to see our grand-mother. We called her Granna. It was a depressing trip too—Granna spent the whole time trying to convince him to get back together with my mother, whom she adored. "Have you talked with Laurel lately?" she'd ask, even way long after the divorce.

I hated hearing her nag him about it; it wasn't like it was in his control anyway. It was humiliating, because it was my mother who had split up with him. It was she who had precipitated the divorce, had pushed the whole thing, I knew that much for sure. My father would have been perfectly content carrying on, living in our blue two-story with Claude and all his books.

My dad once told me that Winston Churchill said that Russia was a riddle, wrapped in a mystery, inside an enigma. According to my dad, Churchill had been talking about my mother. This was before the divorce, and he said it half-bitterly, half-respectfully. Because even when he hated her, he admired her.

I think he would have stayed with her forever, trying to figure out the mystery. He was a puzzle solver, the kind of person who likes theorems, theories. X always had to equal something. It couldn't just be X.

To me, my mother wasn't that mysterious. She was my mother. Always reasonable, always sure of herself. To me, she was about as mysterious as a glass of water. She knew what she wanted; she knew what she didn't want. And that was to be married to my father. I wasn't sure if it was that she fell out of love or if it was that she just never was. In love, I mean.

When we were at Granna's, my mother took off on one of her trips. She'd go to far-off places like Hungary or Alaska. She always went alone. She took pictures, but I never asked to look at them, and she never asked if I wanted to.

chapter *thirteen*

I was sitting in an Adirondack chair eating toast and reading a magazine when my mother came out and joined me. She had that serious look on her face, her look of purpose, the one she got when she wanted to have one of her mother-daughter talks. I dreaded those talks the same way I dreaded my period.

"What are you doing today?" she asked me casually.

I stuffed the rest of my toast into my mouth. "This?"

"Maybe you could get started on your summer reading for AP English," she said, reaching over and brushing some crumbs off my chin.

"Yeah, I was planning on it," I said, even though I hadn't been.

My mother cleared her throat. "Is Conrad doing drugs?" she asked me.

"What?"

"Is Conrad doing drugs?"

I almost choked. "No! Why are you asking me any-way? Conrad doesn't talk to me. Ask Steven."

"I already did. He doesn't know. He wouldn't lie," she said, peering at me.

"Well, I wouldn't either!"

My mother sighed. "I know. Beck's worried. He's been acting differently. He quit football . . ."

"I quit dance," I said, rolling my eyes. "And you don't see me running around with a crack pipe."

She pursed her lips. "Will you promise to tell me if you hear something?"

"I don't know . . . ," I said teasingly. I didn't need to promise her. I knew Conrad wasn't doing drugs. A beer was one thing, but he would never do drugs. I would bet my life on it.

"Belly, this is serious."

"Mom, chill. He's not doing drugs. When'd you turn into such a narc, anyway? You're one to talk." I elbowed her playfully.

She bit back a smile and shook her head. "Don't start."

chapter *fourteen*
AGE 13

The first time they did it, they thought we didn't know. It was actually pretty stupid of them, because it was one of those rare nights when we were all at home. We were in the living room. Conrad was listening to music with his headphones on, and Jeremiah and Steven were playing a video game. I was sitting on the La-Z-Boy reading *Emma*—mostly because I thought it made me look smart, not really because I enjoyed it. If I was reading for real, I would be locked in my room with *Flowers in the Attic* or something and not Jane Austen.

I think Steven smelled it first. He looked around, sniffed like a dog, and then said, "Do you guys smell that?"

"I told you not to eat all those baked beans, Steven," Jeremiah said, his eyes focused on the TV screen.

I snickered. But it wasn't gas; I smelled it too. It was pot. "It's pot," I said, loudly. I wanted to be the one who said it first, to prove how sophisticated and knowledgeable I was.

"No way," said Jeremiah.

Conrad took off his headphones and said, "Belly's right. It's pot."

Steven paused the game and turned to look at me. "How do you know what pot smells like, Belly?" he asked me suspiciously.

"Because, Steven, I get high all the time. I'm a burnout. You didn't know?" I hated it when Steven pulled the big brother routine, especially in front of Conrad and Jeremiah. It was like he was trying to make me feel small on purpose.

He ignored me. "Is that coming from upstairs?"

"It's my mom's," Conrad said, putting his headphones back on again. "For her chemo."

Jeremiah didn't know, I could tell. He didn't say anything, but he looked confused and even hurt, the way he scratched the back of his neck and looked off into space for a minute. Steven and I exchanged a look. It was awkward, whenever Susannah's cancer came up, the two of us being outsiders and all. We never knew what to say, so we didn't say anything. We mostly pretended it wasn't happening, the way Jeremiah did.

My mother didn't, though. She was matter-of-fact,

calm, the way she is about everything. Susannah said my mother made her feel normal. My mother was good at that, making people feel normal. Safe. Like as long as she was there, nothing truly bad could happen.

When they came downstairs a little while later, they were giggling like two teenagers who had snuck into their parents' liquor cabinet. Clearly my mother had partaken in Susannah's stash as well.

Steven and I exchanged another look, this time a horrified one. My mother was probably the last person on earth who would smoke pot, with the exception of our grandmother Gran, her mother.

"Did you kids eat all the Cheetos?" my mother asked, rummaging through a cabinet. "I'm starving."

"Yes," Steven said. He couldn't even look at her.

"What about that bag of Fritos? Get those," Susannah ordered, coming up behind my La-Z-Boy. She touched my hair lightly, which I loved. Susannah was much more affectionate than my mother in those kinds of ways, and she was always calling me the daughter she never had. She loved sharing me with my mother, and my mother didn't mind. Neither did I.

"How are you liking *Emma* so far?" she asked me. Susannah had a way of focusing on you that made you feel like the most interesting person in the room.

I opened my mouth to lie and tell her how great

I thought it was, but before I could, Conrad said very loudly, "She hasn't turned a page in over an hour." He was still wearing his headphones.

I glared at him, but inside I was thrilled that he had noticed. For once, *he* had been watching *me*. But of course he'd noticed—Conrad noticed everything. Conrad would notice if the neighbor's dog had more crust in its right eye than its left, or if the pizza delivery guy was driving a different car. It wasn't really a compliment to be noticed by Conrad. It was a matter of fact.

"You'll love it once it gets going," Susannah assured me, sweeping my bangs across my forehead.

"It always takes me a while to get into a book," I said, in a way that sounded like I was saying sorry. I didn't want her to feel bad, seeing as how she was the one who'd recommended it to me.

Then my mother came into the room with a bag of Twizzlers and the half-eaten bag of Fritos. She tossed a Twizzler at Susannah and said, belatedly, "Catch!"

Susannah reached for it, but it fell on the floor, and she giggled as she picked it up. "Clumsy me," she said, chewing on one end like it was straw and she was a hick. "Whatever has gotten into me?"

"Mom, everyone knows you guys were smoking pot upstairs," Conrad said, just barely bobbing his head to the music that only he could hear.

Susannah covered her mouth with her hand. She didn't say anything, but she looked genuinely upset.

"Whoops," my mother said. "I guess the cat's out of the bag, Beck. Boys, your mother's been taking medicinal marijuana to help with the nausea from her chemo."

Steven didn't look away from the TV when he said, "What about you, Mom? Are you toking up because of your chemo too?"

I knew he was trying to lighten the mood, and it worked. Steven was good at that.

Susannah choked out a laugh, and my mother threw a Twizzler at the back of Steven's head. "Smart-ass. I'm offering up moral support to my best friend in the world. There are worse things."

Steven picked the Twizzler up and dusted it off before popping it into his mouth. "So I guess it's okay with you if I smoke up too?"

"When you get breast cancer," my mother told him, exchanging a smile with Susannah, her best friend in the world.

"Or when your best friend does," Susannah said.

Throughout all of this, Jeremiah wasn't saying anything. He just kept looking at Susannah and then back at the TV, like he was worried she would vanish into thin air while his back was turned.

Our mothers thought we were all at the beach that afternoon. They didn't know that Jeremiah and I had gotten bored and decided to come back to the house for a snack. As we walked up the porch steps, we heard them talking through the window screen.

Jeremiah stopped when he heard Susannah say, "Laur, I hate myself for even thinking this, but I almost think I'd rather die than lose my breast." Jeremiah stopped breathing as he stood there, listening. Then he sat down, and I did too.

My mother said, "I know you don't mean that."

I hated it when my mother said that, and I guessed Susannah did too because she said, "Don't tell me what I mean," and I'd never heard her voice like that before—harsh, angry.

"Okay. Okay. I won't."

Susannah started to cry then. And even though we couldn't see them, I knew that my mother was rubbing Susannah's back in wide circles, the same way she did mine when I was upset.

I wished I could do that for Jeremiah. I knew it would make him feel better, but I couldn't. Instead, I reached over and grabbed his hand and squeezed it tight. He didn't look at me, but he didn't let go either. This was the moment when we became true, real friends.

Then my mother said in her most serious, most deadpan voice, "Your boobs really are pretty goddamn amazing."

Susannah burst out into laughter that sounded like a seal barking, and then she was laughing and crying at the same time. Everything was going to be okay. If my mother was cussing, if Susannah was laughing, it would all be fine.

I let go of Jeremiah's hand and stood up. He did too. We walked back to the beach, neither of us saying anything. What was there to say? "Sorry your mom has cancer"? "I hope she doesn't lose a boob"?

When we got back to our stretch of beach, Conrad and Steven had just come out of the water with their boogie boards. We still weren't saying anything, and Steven noticed. I guessed Conrad did too, but he didn't say anything. It was Steven who said, "What's with you guys?"

"Nothing," I said, pulling my knees to my chest.

"Did you guys just have your first kiss or something?" he said, shaking water off his trunks and onto my knees.

"Shut up," I told him. I was tempted to pants him just to change the subject. The summer before, the boys had gone through an obsession with pantsing one another in public. I had never participated, but at that moment I really wanted to.

"Aww, I knew it!" he said, jabbing me in the shoulder. I shrugged him off and told him to shut up again. He started to sing, "Summer lovin', had me a blast, summer lovin', happened so fast . . ."

"Steven, quit being dumb," I said, turning to shake my head and roll my eyes with Jeremiah.

But then Jeremiah stood up, brushed sand off his shorts, and started walking toward the water and away from us, away from the house.

"Jeremiah, are you on your period or something? I was just kidding, man!" Steven called to him. Jeremiah didn't turn around; he just kept walking down the shore. "Come on!"

"Just leave him alone," Conrad said. The two of them never seemed particularly close, but there were times when I saw how well they understood each other, and this was one of them. Seeing Conrad protective of Jeremiah made me feel this huge surge of love for him—it felt like a wave in my chest washing over me. Which then made me feel guilty, because why should I be feeding into a crush when Susannah had cancer?

I could tell Steven felt bad, and also confused. It was unlike Jeremiah to walk away. He was always the first to laugh, to joke right back.

And because I felt like rubbing salt in the wound, I said, "You're such an asshole, Steven."

Steven gaped at me. "Geez, what did I do?"

I ignored him and fell back onto the towel and closed my eyes. I wished I had Conrad's earphones. I kind of wanted to forget this day ever happened.

Later, when Conrad and Steven decided to go night fishing, Jeremiah declined, even though night fishing was his favorite. He was always trying to get people to go night fishing with him. That night he said he wasn't in the mood. So they left, and Jeremiah stayed behind, with me. We watched TV and played cards. We spent most of the summer doing that, just us. We cemented things between us that summer. He'd wake me up early some mornings, and we would go collect shells or sand crabs, or ride our bikes to the ice cream place three miles away. When it was just us two, he didn't joke around as much, but he was still Jeremiah.

From that summer on I felt closer to Jeremiah than I did to my own brother. Jeremiah was nicer. Maybe because he was somebody's little sibling too, or maybe just because he was that kind of person. He was nice to everybody. He had a talent for making people feel comfortable.

chapter *fifteen*

It had been raining for three days. By four o'clock the third day, Jeremiah was stir-crazy. He wasn't the kind of person to stay inside; he was always moving. Always on his way somewhere new. He said he couldn't take it anymore and asked who wanted to go to the movies. There was only one movie theater in Cousins besides the drive-in, and it was in a mall.

Conrad was in his room, and when Jeremiah went up and asked him to come, he said no. He'd been spending an awful lot of time alone, in his room, and I could tell it hurt Steven's feelings. He'd be leaving soon for a college road trip with our dad, and Conrad didn't seem to care. When Conrad wasn't at work, he was too busy strumming his guitar and listening to music.

So it was just Jeremiah, Steven, and me. I convinced

them to watch a romantic comedy about two dog walkers who walk the same route and fall in love. It was the only thing playing. The next movie wouldn't start for another hour. About five minutes in, Steven stood up, disgusted. "I can't watch this," he said. "You coming, Jere?"

Jeremiah said, "Nah, I'll stay with Belly."

Steven looked surprised. He shrugged and said, "I'll meet you guys when it's over."

I was surprised too. It *was* pretty awful.

Not long after Steven left, a big burly guy sat in the seat right in front of me. "I'll trade you," Jeremiah whispered.

I thought about doing the fake "That's okay" thing but decided against it. This was Jeremiah, after all. I didn't have to be polite. So instead I said thanks and we traded. To see the screen Jeremiah had to keep craning his neck to the right and lean toward me. His hair smelled like Asian pears, this expensive shampoo Susannah used. It was funny. He was this big tall football guy now, and he smelled so sweet. Every time he leaned in, I breathed in the sweet smell of his hair. I wished my hair smelled like that.

Halfway through the movie, Jeremiah got up suddenly. He was gone a few minutes. When he came back, he had a large soda and a pack of Twizzlers. I reached for the soda to take a sip, but there were no straws. "You forgot the straws," I told him.

He ripped the plastic off of the Twizzler box and bit the ends off of two Twizzlers. Then he put them in the cup. He grinned broadly. He looked so proud of himself. I'd forgotten all about our Twizzler straws. We used to do it all the time.

We sipped out of the straws at the same time, like in a 1950s Coke commercial—heads bent, foreheads almost touching. I wondered if people thought we were on a date.

Jeremiah looked at me, and he smiled in this familiar way, and suddenly I had this crazy thought. I thought, *Jeremiah Fisher wants to kiss me.*

Which, was crazy. This was Jeremiah. He'd never looked at me like that, and as for me, Conrad was the one I liked, even when he was moody and inaccessible the way he was now. It had always been Conrad. I'd never seriously considered Jeremiah, not with Conrad standing there. And of course Jeremiah had never looked at me that way before either. I was his pal. His movie-watching partner, the girl he shared a bathroom with, shared secrets with. I wasn't the girl he kissed.

chapter *sixteen*
AGE 14

I knew bringing Taylor was a mistake. I knew it. I knew it and I did it anyway. Taylor Jewel, my best friend. The boys in our grade called her Jewel, which she pretended to hate but secretly loved.

Taylor used to say that every time I came back from the summer house, she had to win me over again. She had to make me want to be there, in my real life with school and school boys and school friends. She'd try to pair me up with the cutest friend of the guy she was obsessed with at the time. I'd go along with it, and maybe we'd go to the movies or to the Waffle House, but I'd never really be there, not completely. Those boys didn't compare to Conrad or Jeremiah, so what was the point?

Taylor was always the pretty one, the one the boys

looked at for that extra beat. I was the funny one, the one who made the boys laugh. I thought that by bringing her I'd be proving that I was a pretty one too. See? See, I'm like her; we are the same. But we weren't, and everybody knew it. I thought that bringing Taylor would guarantee me an invitation to the boys' late-night walks on the boardwalk and their nights on the beach in sleeping bags. I thought it would open up my whole social world that summer, that I would finally, finally be in the thick of things.

I was right about that part at least.

Taylor had been begging me to bring her for forever. I'd resisted her, saying it'd be too crowded, but she was very persuasive. It was my own fault. I'd bragged about the boys too much. And deep down, I did want her there. She was my best friend, after all. She hated that we didn't share everything—every moment, every experience. When she joined the Spanish club, she insisted I join too, even though I didn't take Spanish. "For when we go to Cabo after graduation," she said. I wanted to go to the Galápagos Islands for graduation, that was my dream. I wanted to see a blue-footed booby. My dad said he'd take me too. I didn't tell Taylor, though. She wouldn't like it.

My mother and I picked Taylor up at the airport. She walked off the plane in a pair of short shorts and a tank top I'd never seen before. Hugging her, I tried not to sound jealous when I said, "When'd you get that?"

"My mom took me shopping for beach stuff right before I left," she said, handing me one of her duffel bags. "Cute, right?"

"Yeah, cute." Her bag was heavy. I wondered if she'd forgotten she was only staying a week.

"She feels bad she and Daddy are getting a divorce so she's buying me all kinds of stuff," Taylor continued, rolling her eyes. "We even got mani-pedis together. Look!" Taylor lifted up her right hand. Her nails were painted a raspberry color, and they were long and square.

"Are those real?"

"Yeah! Duh. I don't wear fake, Belly."

"But I thought you had to keep your nails short for violin."

"Oh, that. Mommy finally let me quit violin. Divorce guilt," she said knowingly. "You know how it is."

Taylor was the only girl I knew our age who still called her mother Mommy. She was the only one who could get away with it too.

The boys came to attention right away. Right away they looked at her, checked out her smallish B-cups and her blond hair. It's a Miracle Bra, I wanted to tell them. That's half a bottle of Sun-In. Her hair isn't usually that yellow. Not that they would've cared either way.

My brother, on the other hand, barely looked up from the TV. Taylor irritated him, always had. I wondered if he'd already warned Conrad and Jeremiah about her.

"Hi, Ste-ven," she said in a singsong voice.

"Hey," he mumbled.

Taylor looked at me and crossed her eyes. *Grump*, she mouthed, emphasis on the *p*.

I laughed. "Taylor, this is Conrad and Jeremiah. Steven you know." I was curious about who she'd pick, who she'd think was cuter, funnier. Better.

"Hey," she said, sizing them up, and right away I could tell Conrad was the one. And I was glad. Because I knew that Conrad would never, ever go for her.

"Hey," they said.

Then Conrad turned back to the TV just like I knew he would. Jeremiah treated her to one of his lop-sided smiles and said, "So you're Belly's friend, huh? We thought she didn't have any friends."

I waited for him to grin at me to show he was just joking, but he didn't even look my way. "Shut up, Jeremiah," I said, and he grinned at me then, but it was a quick cursory one, and he went right back to looking at Taylor.

"Belly has tons of friends," Taylor informed him in her breezy way. "Do I look like someone who would hang with a loser?"

"Yes," my brother said from the couch. His head popped up. "You do."

Taylor glared at him. "Go back to jacking off, Steven." She turned to me and said, "Why don't you show me our room?"

"Yes, why don't you do that, Belly? Why don't you go be Tay-Tay's slave?" Steven said. Then he lay back down again.

I ignored him. "Come on, Taylor."

As soon as we got to my room, Taylor flung herself onto the bed by the window, my bed, the one I always slept in. "Oh my God, he is so cute."

"Which one?" I said, even though I knew.

"The dark one, of course. I love my men dark."

Inwardly I rolled my eyes. Men? Taylor had only ever gone out with two boys, neither of them anything close to being men.

"I doubt it will happen," I told her. "Conrad doesn't care about girls." I knew that wasn't true; he did care about girls. He'd cared enough about that girl Angie from last summer to go to second with her, hadn't he?

Taylor's brown eyes gleamed. "I love a challenge. Didn't I win class president last year? And class secretary the year before that?"

"Of course I remember. I was your campaign manager. But Conrad's different. He's . . ." I hesitated, searching for just the right word to scare Taylor off. "Almost, like, disturbed."

"What?" she shrieked.

Quickly I backtracked. Maybe "disturbed" had been too strong a word. "I don't mean "disturbed," exactly, but he can be really intense. Serious. You should go for

Jeremiah. I think he's more your type."

"And just what does that mean, Belly?" Taylor demanded. "That I'm not deep?"

"Well—" She was about as deep as an inflatable kiddie pool.

"Don't answer that." Taylor opened up her duffel bag and started pulling things out. "Jeremiah is cute, but Conrad's the one I want. I am gonna make that boy's head spin."

"Don't say I didn't warn you." I was already looking forward to saying I told you so, whenever that moment should arrive. Hopefully sooner than later.

She lifted up a yellow polka-dot bikini. "Itsy-bitsy enough for Conrad, do you think?"

"That bikini wouldn't fit Bridget," I said. Her little sister Bridget was seven, and she was small for her age.

"Exactly."

I rolled my eyes. "Don't say I didn't warn you. And that's my bed you're sitting on."

The two of us changed into our suits right away— Taylor into her tiny yellow bikini and me into my black tankini with the support bra and the really high neckline. As we changed, she looked me over and said, "Belly, your boobs have really gotten big!"

I threw my T-shirt over my head and said, "Not really."

But it was true, they had. Overnight, almost. I didn't

have them the summer before, that was for sure. I hated them. They slowed me down: I couldn't run fast anymore—it was too embarrassing. It was why I wore baggy T-shirts and one-pieces. I couldn't stand to hear what the boys would say about it. They would tease me for sure, and Steven would tell me to go put some clothes on, which would make me want to die.

"What size are you now?" she asked accusingly.

"B," I lied. It was more like a C.

Taylor looked relieved. "Oh, well we're still the same, then, because I'm practically a B. Why don't you wear one of my bikinis? You look like you're trying out for the swim team in that one-piece." She lifted up a blue-and-white striped one with red bows on the sides.

"I *am* on the swim team," I reminded her. I'd done winter swim with my neighborhood swim team. I couldn't compete in summer because I was always at Cousins. Being on the swim team made me feel connected to my summer life, like it was just a matter of time before I was at the beach again.

"Ugh, don't remind me," Taylor said. She dangled the bikini from side to side. "This would be *so* cute on you, with your brown hair and your new boobs."

I made a face and pushed the bikini away.

Part of me did want to show off and wow them with how much I had grown, how I was a real girl now, but the other more sane part knew it would be a death wish.

Steven would throw a towel over my head, and I would feel ten years old again instead of thirteen.

"But why?"

"I like to do laps in the pool," I said. Which was true. I did.

She shrugged. "Okay, but don't blame me when the guys don't talk to you."

I shrugged right back at her. "I don't care if they talk to me or not, I don't think of them that way."

"Yeah, right! You've been, like, obsessed with Conrad for as long as I've known you! You wouldn't even talk to any of the guys at school last year."

"Taylor, that was a really long time ago. They're like brothers to me, just like Steven," I said, pulling on a pair of gym shorts. "Talk to them all you want."

The truth was, I liked both of them in different ways and I didn't want her to know, because whichever guy she picked would feel like a leftover. And it wasn't like it would sway Taylor. She was going for Conrad either way. I wanted to tell her, Anyone but Conrad, but it wouldn't be true, not completely. I would be jealous if she picked Jeremiah, too, because he was *my* friend, not hers.

It took Taylor forever to pick out a pair of sunglasses that matched her bikini (she'd brought four pairs), plus two magazines and her suntan oil. By the time we got outside, the boys were already in the pool.

I threw my clothes off right away, ready to jump in,

but Taylor hesitated, her Polo towel tight around her shoulders. I could tell she was suddenly nervous about her itsy-bitsy bikini, and I was glad. I was getting a little bit sick of her showing off.

The boys didn't even look over. I had been worried that with Taylor there they might not want to do all the usual stuff, that they might act differently. But there they were, dunking one another for all it was worth.

Kicking off my flip-flops, I said, "Let's get in the pool."

"I might lay out for a little bit first," Taylor said. She finally dropped her towel and spread it out on a lounge chair. "Don't you want to lay out too?"

"No. It's hot and I want to swim. Besides, I'm already tan." And I was. I was turning the color of dark toffee. I looked like a whole different person in the summer, which might have been the best part of it.

Taylor on the other hand was pasty and bright like biscuit dough. I had a feeling she'd catch up with me fast, though. She was good at that.

I took off my glasses and set them on top of my clothes. Then I walked over to the deep end and jumped right in. The water felt like a shock to the system, in the best way possible. When I came up for air, I treaded water over to the boys. "Let's play Marco Polo," I said.

Steven, who was busy trying to dunk Conrad, stopped and said, "Marco Polo's boring."

"Let's play chicken," Jeremiah suggested.

"What's that?" I said.

"It's when two teams of people climb up on each other's shoulders and you try to push the other person down," my brother explained.

"It's fun, I swear," Jeremiah assured me. Then he called over to Taylor, "Tyler, you wanna play chicken with us? Or are you too chicken?"

Taylor looked up from her magazine. I couldn't see her eyes because of her sunglasses, but I knew she was annoyed. "It's Tay-lor, not Tyler, Jeremy. And no, I don't want to play."

Steven and Conrad exchanged a look. I knew what they were thinking. "Come on, Taylor, it'll be fun," I said, rolling my eyes. "Don't be a chicken."

She made a big show of sighing, and then she put her magazine down and stood up, smoothing down her bikini in the back. "Do I have to take my sunglasses off?"

Jeremiah grinned at her. "Not if you're on my team. You won't be falling off."

Taylor took them off anyway, and I realized then that the teams were uneven, and someone would have to sit out. "I'll watch," I offered, even though I wanted to play.

"That's okay. I won't play," Conrad said.

"We'll play two rounds," said Steven.

Conrad shrugged. "That's all right." He swam over to the side of the pool.

"I call Tay-lor," Jeremiah announced.

"No fair; she's lighter," Steven argued. Then he looked over and saw the expression on my face. "It's just that you're taller than her is all."

I didn't want to play anymore. "Why don't I just sit out, then? I'd hate to break your back, Steven."

Jeremiah said, "Aw, I'll take you, Belly. We'll take those guys down. I think you're probably a lot tougher than little Tay-lor."

Taylor walked down the steps and into the pool slowly, cringing at the temperature. "I'm very tough, Jeremy," she said.

Then Jeremiah crouched down in the water, and I scrambled to get onto his shoulders. He was slippery, so it was hard to stay on at first. Then he stood up and righted himself.

I shifted and balanced my hands on his head. "Am I too heavy?" I asked him quietly. He was so wiry and thin, I was afraid I'd break him.

"You weigh, like, nothing," he lied, breathing hard and gripping on to my legs.

I wanted to kiss the top of his head right then.

Across from us Taylor was perched on top of Steven's shoulders giggling and pulling his hair to hold herself steady. Steven looked like he was ready to pitch her off of him and across the pool.

"Ready?" Jeremiah asked. In a low voice he said to me, "The trick is to just keep steady."

Steven nodded, and we waddled over to the middle of the pool.

Conrad, who was treading over by the side, said, "Ready, set, go."

Taylor and I stretched our arms out to each other, pushing and shoving. She couldn't stop giggling, and when I gave her one strong push, she said, "Oh, shit!" and they both fell backward.

Jeremiah and I burst out laughing and high-fived each other. When they resurfaced, Steven glared at Taylor and said, "I told you to hold on tight."

She splashed him right in the face and said, "I was!" Her eyeliner was smudged and her mascara was starting to run. She still looked pretty, though.

Jeremiah said, "Belly?"

I said, "Hmm?" I was starting to get pretty comfortable up there, so high.

"Watch out." Then he lurched forward, and I was flying into the water, and so was he. I couldn't stop laughing, and I swallowed about a jugful of water, but I didn't care.

When both of our heads popped up, I went straight for his and took him by surprise with a good dunk.

Then Taylor said, "Let's play again. I'll be with Jeremy this time. Steven, you can be Belly's partner."

Steven still looked grumpy, and he said, "Con, take my spot."

"All right," Conrad said, but his voice said he didn't want to at all.

When he swam over to me, I said defensively, "I'm not that heavy."

"I never said you were." Then he stooped in front of me, and I climbed on top. His shoulders were more muscular than Jeremiah's, more weighty. "You okay up there?"

"Yeah."

Across from us Taylor was having trouble getting onto Jeremiah's shoulders. She kept slipping right off and laughing. They were having a lot of fun. Too much fun. I watched them jealously, and I almost forgot to be aware of the fact that Conrad was holding on to my legs, and as far as I could remember, he had never so much as accidentally grazed my knee before.

"Let's hurry up and play," I said. My voice sounded jealous even to my own ears. I hated that.

Conrad had less trouble moving into the center of the pool. I was kind of surprised by how easily he moved around with my extra weight around his shoulders.

"Ready?" Conrad said to Jeremiah and Taylor, who had finally managed to stay put.

"Yes!" Taylor shouted.

In my head I said, *You're going down, Jewel.* "Yes," I said out loud.

I leaned forward and used both of my hands to give

her a hard push. She swayed to the side but stayed on, and said, "Hey!"

I smiled. "Hey," I said, and pushed her again.

Taylor narrowed her eyes and pushed me back, hard but not hard enough.

Then we were both pushing at each other, only this time it was so much easier because I felt steady. I pushed her once, firmly, and she tipped forward, but Jeremiah was still standing. I clapped loudly. This was pretty fun.

I was surprised when Conrad held out his hand for a high five. He wasn't a high five kind of person.

When Taylor resurfaced this time, she wasn't laughing. Her blond hair was matted to her head, and she said, "This game sucks. I don't want to play anymore."

"Sore loser," I said, and Conrad lowered me into the water.

"Nice job," he said, giving me one of his rare smiles. I felt like I had won the lottery from that one smile.

"I play to win," I told him. I knew he did too.

chapter *seventeen*

A few days after we shared Twizzlers at the movies, Jeremiah announced, "I'm gonna teach Belly how to drive stick shift today."

"Do you mean it?" I said eagerly. It was a clear day; the first all week. A perfect day for driving. It was Jeremiah's day off, and I couldn't believe he was willing to spend it teaching me how to drive stick. I'd been begging him since last year to teach me—Steven had tried and had given up after our third lesson.

Steven shook his head and took a swig of orange juice from the carton on the table. "Do you want to die, man? Because Belly will kill you both, not to mention your clutch. Don't do it. I'm telling you this as your friend."

"Shut up, Steven!" I yelled, kicking him under the

table. "Just 'cause you're a terrible teacher . . ." Steven had refused to get into a car with me again after I'd accidentally gotten a teeny-tiny dent in his fender when he was teaching me how to parallel park.

"I'm confident in my teaching skills," Jeremiah said. "By the time I'm finished with her, she'll be better than you."

Steven snorted. "Good luck." Then he frowned. "How long are you gonna be gone? I thought we were going to the driving range."

"You could come with us," I offered.

Steven ignored me and said to Jeremiah, "You need to practice your swing, dude."

I glanced at Jeremiah, who looked at me and hesitated. "I'll be back by lunch. We can go after," he said.

Steven rolled his eyes. "Fine." I could tell he was annoyed and a little hurt, which made me feel both smug and sorry for him. He wasn't used to being left out of things the way I was.

We went out to practice on the road that led down to the other side of the beach. It was quiet. There was no one else out on the road, just us. We listened to Jeremiah's old *Nevermind* CD from a million years ago.

"It's hot when a girl can drive stick," Jeremiah explained above Kurt Cobain. "It shows she's confident, she knows what she's doing."

I put the car into first gear and eased my foot off the

clutch. "I thought boys liked it when girls were helpless."

"They like that too. But I just happen to prefer smart, confident girls."

"Bull. You liked Taylor, and she's not like that."

He groaned and stuck his arm out the window. "Do you have to bring that up again?"

"I'm just saying. She wasn't that smart and confident."

"Maybe not, but she definitely knew what she was doing," he said, before exploding into laughter.

I hit him on the arm, hard. "You're so gross," I said. "And you're also a liar. I know for a fact that you guys didn't even get to second."

He stopped laughing. "Okay, fine. We didn't. But she was a good kisser. She tasted like Skittles."

Taylor loved Skittles. She was always popping them into her mouth, like vitamins, like they were good for her. I wondered how I'd stacked up against Taylor, if he thought I'd been a good kisser too.

I sneaked a peek at him, and he must have seen it on my face, because he laughed and said, "But you, you were the best, Bells."

I punched him on the arm, and even then he didn't stop laughing. He just laughed harder. "Don't take your foot off the clutch," he said, gasping with laughter.

I was kind of surprised he even remembered. I mean,

it had been memorable for me, but it had been my first kiss and it had been *Jeremiah*. But the fact that he remembered, that sort of made his laughing okay.

"You were my first kiss," I said. I felt like I could say anything to him at that moment. It felt like how it used to be with us before we grew up and things got complicated. It felt easy and friendly and normal.

He looked away, embarrassed. "Yeah, I know."

"How did you know?" I demanded. Had I been that awful at kissing that he'd suspected? How humiliating.

"Um, Taylor told me. Afterward."

"What! I can't believe she did that. That Judas!" I almost stopped the car. Actually, I could believe it. But it still felt like a betrayal.

"It's no big deal." But his cheeks were patchy and pink. "I mean, the first time I kissed a girl was a joke. She kept telling me I was doing it wrong."

"Who? Who was your first kiss?"

"You don't know her. It doesn't matter."

"Come on," I wheedled. "Tell me."

We stalled out then, and Jeremiah said, "Just put your foot on the clutch and put it in neutral."

"Not until you tell me."

"Fine. It was Christi Turnduck," he said, ducking his head.

"You kissed Turducken?" Now I was laughing. I did so know Christi Turnduck. She used to be a Cousins Beach regular just like us, only she lived there year round.

"She had a big crush on me," Jeremiah said, shrugging his shoulders.

"Did you tell Con and Steven?"

"Hell, no, I didn't tell them I kissed Turducken!" he said. "And you better not either! Pinky promise."

I offered him my pinky, and we shook on it.

"Christi Turnduck. She did kiss nice. She taught me everything I know. I wonder what ever happened to her."

I wondered if Turducken had been a better kisser than me too. She must have been, if she had taught Jeremiah.

We stalled out again. "This sucks. I quit."

"There's no quitting in driving," Jeremiah ordered. "Come on."

I sighed and started the car up again. Two hours later, I had it. Sort of. I still stalled out, but I was getting somewhere. I was driving. Jeremiah said I was a natural.

By the time we got back to the house, it was after four and Steven had left. I guessed he'd gotten tired of waiting and had gone to the driving range by himself. My mother and Susannah were watching old movies in Susannah's room. It was dark, and they had the curtains drawn.

I stood outside their door a minute, listening to them laugh. I felt left out. I envied their relationship. They were exactly like copilots, in perfect balance. I didn't have that kind of friendship, the forever kind of friendship that will last your whole life through, no matter what.

I walked into the room, and Susannah said, "Belly! Come watch movies with us."

I crawled into bed in between the two of them. Lying on the bed in the semi-dark, it felt cozy, like we were in a cave. "Jeremiah's been teaching me how to drive," I told them.

"Darling boy," Susannah said, smiling faintly.

"Brave, too," my mother said. She tweaked my nose.

I snuggled under the comforter. He *was* pretty great. It had been nice of him to take me out driving when no one else would. Just because I'd banged up the car a few times, it didn't mean that I wasn't going to end up being an excellent driver like everyone else. Thanks to him, I could drive stick now. I was going to be one of those confident girls, the kind who knows what she's doing. When I got my license, I would drive up to Susannah's house and take Jeremiah for a drive, to thank him.

chapter *eighteen*
AGE 14

After Taylor got out of the shower, she started rummaging through her duffel bag and I lay on my bed and watched her. She pulled out three different sundresses—one white eyelet, one Hawaiian print, and one black linen. "Which one should I wear tonight?" she asked me. She asked the question like it was a test.

I was tired of her tests and having to prove myself all the time. I said, "We're just eating dinner, Taylor. We're not going anywhere special."

She shook her head at me, and the towel on her head bounced back and forth. "We're going to the boardwalk tonight, though, remember? We have to look cute for that. There'll be boys there. Let me pick out your outfit, okay?"

It used to be that when Taylor picked out my clothes, I felt like the nerdy girl transformed at the prom, in a good way. Now it felt like I was her clueless mom who didn't know how to dress right.

I hadn't brought any dresses with me. In fact, I never had. I never even thought to. I only had two dresses at home—one my grandmother bought me for Easter and one I had to buy for eighth-grade graduation. Nothing seemed to fit me right lately. Things were either too long in the crotch or too tight in the waist. I had never thought much about dresses, but looking at hers all laid out on the bed like that, I was jealous.

"I'm not getting dressed up for the boardwalk," I told her.

"Let me just see what you have," she said, walking over to my closet.

"Taylor, I said no! This is what I'm wearing." I gestured at my cutoff shorts and Cousins Beach T-shirt.

Taylor made a face, but she backed away from my closet and went back to her three sundresses. "Fine. Have it your way, grumpy. Now, which one should I wear?"

I sighed. "The black one," I said, closing my eyes. "Now hurry up and put some clothes on."

Dinner that night was scallops and asparagus. When my mother cooked, it was always some sort of seafood with lemon and olive oil and a vegetable. Every time. Susannah only cooked every once in a while, so besides the first night, which was always bouillabaisse, you never knew what you were going to get. She might spend the whole afternoon puttering around the kitchen, making something I'd never had before, like Moroccan chicken with figs. She'd pull out her spiral bound Junior League cookbook that had buttery pages and notes in the margins, the one my mother made fun of. Or she might make American cheese omelets with ketchup and toast. Us kids were supposedly in charge of one night a week too, and that usually meant hamburgers or frozen pizza. But most nights, we ate whatever we wanted, whenever we felt like eating. I loved that about the summer house. At home, we had dinner every night at six thirty, like clockwork. Here, it was like everything just kind of relaxed, even my mother.

Taylor leaned forward and said, "Laurel, what's the craziest thing you and Susannah did when you were our age?" Taylor talked to people like she was at a slumber party, always. Adults, boys, the cafeteria lady, everyone.

My mother and Susannah looked at each other and smiled. They knew, but they weren't telling. My mother wiped her mouth with her napkin and said, "We snuck onto the golf course one night and planted daisies."

I knew that wasn't the truth, but Steven and Jeremiah laughed. Steven said in his annoying know-it-all kind of way, "You guys were boring even when you were teenagers."

"*I* think it's really sweet," Taylor said, squirting a glob of ketchup onto her plate. Taylor ate everything with ketchup—eggs, pizza, pasta, everything.

Conrad, who I thought hadn't even been listening, said, "You guys are lying. That wasn't the craziest thing you ever did."

Susannah put her hands up, like, *I surrender.* "Mothers get to have secrets too," she said. "I don't ask you boys about your secrets, now, do I?"

"Yes, you do," said Jeremiah. He pointed his fork at her. "You ask all the time. If I had a journal, you would read it."

"No, I wouldn't," she protested.

My mother said, "Yes, you would."

Susannah glared at my mother. "I would never." Then she looked at Conrad and Jeremiah sitting next to each other. "Fine, I might, but only Conrad's. He's so good at keeping everything locked inside, I never know what he's thinking. But not you, Jeremiah. You, my baby boy, wear your heart right here." She reached over and touched his sweatshirt sleeve.

"No, I don't," he protested, stabbing a scallop on his plate. "I have secrets."

That's when Taylor said, "Sure you do, Jeremy," in this really sickeningly flirtatious way.

He grinned at her, which made me want to choke on my asparagus.

That's when *I* said, "Taylor and I are going to go to the boardwalk tonight. Will one of you guys drop us off?"

Before my mother or Susannah could answer, Jeremiah said, "Ooh, the boardwalk. I think we should go to the boardwalk too." Turning to Conrad and Steven, he added, "Right, guys?" Normally I would have been thrilled that any of them wanted to go somewhere I was going, but not this time. I knew it wasn't for me.

I looked at Taylor, who was suddenly busy cutting up her scallops into tiny bite-size pieces. She knew it was for her too.

"The boardwalk sucks," said Steven.

Conrad said, "Not interested."

"Who invited you guys anyway?" I said.

Steven rolled his eyes. "No one invites anyone to the boardwalk. You just go. It's a free country."

"Is it a free country?" my mother mused. "I want you to really think about that statement, Steven. What about our civil liberties? Are we really free if—"

"Laurel, please," Susannah said, shaking her head. "Let's not talk politics at the dinner table."

"I don't know of a better time for political discourse," my mother said calmly. Then she looked at me. I mouthed, *Please stop*, and she sighed. It was better to stop her right away before she really got going. "Okay, fine. Fine. No more politics. I'm going to the bookstore downtown. I'll drop you guys off on the way."

"Thanks, Mom," I said. "It'll be just Taylor and me."

Jeremiah ignored me and turned to Steven and Conrad. "Come on, guys," he said. "It'll be *amazing*." Taylor had been calling everything amazing all day.

"Fine, but I'm going to the arcade," said Steven.

"Con?" Jeremiah looked at Conrad, who shook his head.

"Come on, *Con*," Taylor said, poking at him with her fork. "Come with us."

He shook his head, and Taylor made a face. "Fine. We'll be sure to have lots of fun without you."

Jeremiah said, "Don't worry about him. He's gonna have lots of fun here, reading the Encyclopaedia Britannica." Conrad ignored this, but Taylor giggled and tucked her hair behind her ears, which is when I knew that she liked Jeremiah now.

Then Susannah said, "Don't leave without some money for ice cream." I could tell she was happy we were all hanging out, except for Conrad, who seemed to prefer hanging out by himself this summer. Nothing made Susannah happier than thinking up activities for us kids to do. I think that she would have made a really good camp director.

In the car we waited for my mother and the boys to come out, and I whispered, "I thought you liked Conrad."

Taylor rolled her eyes. "Blah. He's boring. I think I'll like Jeremy instead."

"His name is Jeremiah," I said sourly.

"I *know* that." Then she looked at me, and her eyes widened. "Why, do you like him now?"

"No!"

She let out an impatient breath of air. "Belly, you've got to pick one. You can't have them both."

"I know that," I snapped. "And for your information, I don't want either of them. It's not like they look at me like that anyway. They look at me like Steven does. Like a little sister."

Taylor tugged at my T-shirt collar. "Well, maybe if you showed a little cleave . . ."

I shrugged her hand away. "I'm not showing any 'cleave.' And I told you I don't like either of them. Not anymore."

"So you don't care that I'm going after Jeremy?" she asked. I could tell the only reason she was asking was so she could absolve herself of any future guilt. Not that she would even feel guilty.

So I said, "If I told you I cared, would you stop?"

She thought for, like, a second. "Probably. If you really, really cared. But then I would just go after Conrad. I'm here to have fun, Belly."

I sighed. At least she was honest. I wanted to say, I thought you were here to have fun with *me*. But I didn't.

"Go after him," I told her. "I don't care."

Taylor wiggled her eyebrows at me, her old trademark move. "Yay! It is *so* on."

"Wait." I grabbed her wrist. "Promise me you'll be nice to him."

"Of course I'll be nice. I'm always nice." She patted me on the shoulder. "You're such a worrier, Belly. I told you, I just want to have fun."

That's when my mother and the boys came out, and for the first time there was no fight over shotgun. Jeremiah gave it over to Steven easily.

When we got to the boardwalk, Steven headed straight for the arcade and spent the whole night there. Jeremiah walked around with us, and he even rode the carousel, even though I knew he thought it was lame. He got all stretched out on the sleigh and pretended to take a nap while Taylor and I bounced up and down on horses, mine a blond palomino and hers a black stallion. (*Black Beauty* was still her favorite book, although she'd never admit it.) Then Taylor made him win her a stuffed Tweety Bird with the quarter toss. Jeremiah was a pro at the quarter toss. The Tweety Bird was huge, almost as tall as she was. He carried it for her.

I should never have gone along. I could have predicted the whole night, right down to how invisible I'd feel. All the time I wished I was at home, listening to Conrad play the guitar through my bedroom wall, or watching Woody Allen movies with Susannah and my mother. And I didn't even like Woody Allen. I wondered if this was how the rest of the week was going to be. I'd forgotten that about Taylor, the way she got when she wanted something—driven, single-minded, and determined as all get-out. She'd just arrived, and already she'd forgotten about me.

chapter *nineteen*

We'd only just gotten there, and it was already time for Steven to go. He and our dad were going on their college road trip, and instead of coming back to Cousins after, he was going home. Supposedly to start studying for the SATs, but more likely, to hang out with his new girlfriend.

I went to his room to watch him pack up. He hadn't brought much, just a duffel bag. I was suddenly sad to see him leave. Without Steven everything would be off balance—he was the buffer, the real life reminder that nothing really changes, that everything can stay the same. Because, Steven never changed. He was just obnoxious, insufferable Steven, my big brother, the bane of my existence. He was like our old flannel blanket that smelled like wet dog—smelly, comforting, a part of the infrastructure that made up my world. And with him there, everything would still be the same, three against one, boys against girls.

"I wish you weren't leaving," I said, tucking my knees into my chest.

"I'll see you in a month," he reminded me.

"A month and a half," I corrected him sullenly. "You're missing my birthday, you know."

"I'll give you your present when I see you at home."

"Not the same." I knew I was being a baby, but I couldn't help it. "Will you at least send me a postcard?"

Steven zipped up his duffel bag. "I doubt I'll have time. I'll send you a text, though."

"Will you bring me back a Princeton sweatshirt?" I couldn't wait to wear a college sweatshirt. They were like a badge that said you were mature, practically college age if not already. I wished I had a whole drawer full of them.

"If I remember," he said.

"I'll remind you," I said. "I'll text you."

"Okay. It'll be your birthday present."

"Deal." I fell back onto his bed and pushed my feet up against his wall. He hated it when I did that. "I'll probably miss you, a little bit."

"You'll be too busy drooling over Conrad to notice I'm gone," Steven said.

I stuck my tongue out at him.

Steven left really early the next morning. Conrad and Jeremiah were going to drive him to the airport. I went down to say good-bye, but I didn't try to go along because I knew he wouldn't want me to. He wanted some time, just them, and for once I was going to let him have it without a fight.

When he hugged me good-bye, he gave me his trademark condescending look—sad eyes and a half grimace— and said, "Don't do anything stupid, all right?" He said it in this really meaningful way, like he was trying to tell me something important, like I was supposed to understand.

But I didn't. I said, "Don't you do anything stupid either, butthead."

He sighed and shook his head at me like I was a child.

I tried not to let it bother me. After all, he was leaving, and things wouldn't be the same without him. At the very least I could send him off without getting into a petty argument. "Tell Dad I said hi," I said.

I didn't go back to bed right away. I stayed on the front porch awhile, feeling blue and a little teary—not that I would ever admit it to Steven.

In a lot of ways it was like the last summer. That fall, Conrad would start college. He was going to Brown. He might not come back next summer. He might have an internship, or summer school, or he might backpack across Europe with all his new dorm buddies. And Jeremiah, he might go to the football camp he was always talking about. There were a lot of things that could happen between now and then. It occurred to me that I was going to have to make the most of this summer, really make it count, in case there wasn't another one quite like it. After all, I would be sixteen soon. I was getting older too. Things couldn't stay the same forever.

chapter *twenty*
AGE II

The four of us were lying on a big blanket in the sand. Conrad, Steven, Jeremiah, and then me on the edge. That was my spot. When they let me come along. This was one of those rare days.

It was already midafternoon, so hot my hair felt like it was on fire, and they were playing cards while I listened in.

Jeremiah said, "Would you rather be boiled in olive oil or skinned alive with a burning hot butter knife?"

"Olive oil," said Conrad confidently. "It's over quicker."

"Olive oil," I echoed.

"Butter knife," said Steven. "There's more of a chance I can turn the tables on the guy and skin *him*."

"That wasn't an option," Conrad told him. "It's a question about death, not turning the tables on somebody."

"Fine. Olive oil," Steven said grumpily. "What about you, Jeremiah?"

"Olive oil," Jeremiah said. "Now you go, Con."

Conrad squinted his eyes up at the sun and said, "Would you rather live one perfect day over and over or live your life with no perfect days but just decent ones?"

Jeremiah didn't say anything for a minute. He loved this game. He loved to mull over the different possibilities. "With that one perfect day, would I know I was reliving it, like *Groundhog Day*?"

"No."

"Then I'll take the perfect day," he decided.

"Well, if the perfect day involves—," Steven began, but then he looked over at me and stopped speaking, which I hated. "I'll take the perfect day too."

"Belly?" Conrad looked at me. "What would you pick?"

My mind raced around in circles as I tried to find the right answer. "Um. I'd take living my life with decent days. That way I could still hope for that one perfect day," I said. "I wouldn't want to have a life that's just one day over and over."

"Yeah, but you wouldn't know it," Jeremiah argued.

I shrugged. "But you might, deep down."

"That's stupid," Steven said.

"I don't think it's stupid. I think I agree with her." Conrad gave me this look, the kind of look I bet soldiers give each other when they're teaming up against somebody else. It was like we were in it together.

I gave Steven a little shimmy. I couldn't help myself. "See?" I said. "Conrad agrees with me."

Steven mimicked, "Conrad agrees with me. Conrad loves me. Conrad's *awesome*—"

"Shut up, Steven!" I yelled.

He grinned and said, "My turn to ask a question. Belly, would you rather eat mayonnaise every day, or be flatchested for the rest of your life?"

I turned on my side, grabbed a handful of sand, and threw it at Steven. He was in the middle of laughing, and a bunch got in his mouth and stuck to his wet cheeks. He screamed, "You're dead, Belly!"

Then he lunged at me, and I rolled away from him. "Leave me alone," I said defiantly. "You can't hurt me or I'll tell Mom."

"You're such a pain in the ass," he spat out, grabbing my leg roughly. "I'm throwing you in the water."

I tried to shake him off, but I only succeeded in kicking more sand into his face. Which of course only made him madder.

Conrad said, "Leave her alone, Steven. Let's go swim."

"Yeah, come on," said Jeremiah.

Steven hesitated. "Fine," he said, spitting out sand. "But you're still dead, Belly." He pointed at me, and then made a cutting motion with his finger.

I gave him the finger and flipped over, but inside I was shaking. Conrad had defended me. Conrad cared whether or not I was dead.

Steven was mad at me the whole rest of the day, but it was worth it. It was also ironic, Steven teasing me about being flat-chested, because two summers later I had to wear a bra, but, like, for real.

chapter *twenty-one*

The night Steven left, I headed down to the pool for one of my midnight swims, and Conrad and Jeremiah and this neighbor guy Clay Bertolet were sitting on the lounge chairs drinking beer. Clay lived way down the street, and he'd been coming to Cousins Beach for almost as long as we had. He was a year older than Conrad. No one had even liked him much. He was just a person to hang out with, I guess.

Right away I stiffened and held my beach towel closer to my chest. I wondered if I should turn back. Clay had always made me nervous. I didn't have to swim that night. I could do it the next night. But no, I had as much right to be out there as they did. More, even.

I walked over to them, pretend-confident. "Hey, guys," I said. I didn't let go of my towel. It felt funny to be standing there in a towel and a bikini when they were all wearing clothes.

Clay looked up at me, his eyes narrow. "Hey, Belly. Long time no see." He patted the lounge chair. "Sit down."

I hated when people said "long time no see." It was such a dumb way to say hello. But I sat down anyway.

He leaned in and gave me a hug. He smelled like beer and Polo Sport. "So how've you been?" he asked.

Before I could answer, Conrad said, "She's fine, and now it's time for bed. Good night, Belly."

I tried not to sound like a five-year-old when I said, "I'm not going to sleep yet, I'm swimming."

"You should head back up," Jeremiah said, putting his beer down. "Your mom will kill you for drinking."

."Hello. I'm not drinking," I reminded him.

Clay offered me his Corona. "Here," he said, winking. He seemed drunk.

I hesitated, and Conrad snapped irritably, "Don't give her that. She's a kid, for God's sake."

I glared at him. "Quit acting like Steven." For a second or two I considered taking Clay's beer. It would be my first. But then I'd only be doing it to spite Conrad, and I wasn't going to let him control what I did.

"No, thanks," I told him.

Conrad nodded imperceptibly. "Now go back to bed like a good girl."

It felt just like when he and Steven and Jeremiah used to leave me out of things on purpose. I could feel my cheeks burning as I said, "I'm only two years younger than you."

"Two and a quarter," he corrected automatically.

Clay laughed, and I could smell his yeasty breath. "Shit, my girlfriend was fifteen." Then he looked at me. "Ex-girlfriend."

I smiled weakly. Inside, I was shrinking away from him and his breath. But the way Conrad was watching us, well, I liked it. I liked taking his friend away from him, even if it was just for five minutes. "Isn't that, like, illegal?" I asked Clay.

He laughed again. "You're cute, Belly."

I could feel myself blush. "So, um, why did you break up?" I asked, like I didn't already know. They broke up because Clay's a jerk, that was why. Clay had always been a jerk. He used to try to feed the seagulls Alka-Seltzer because he heard it made their stomachs blow up.

Clay scratched the back of his neck. "I don't know. She had to go to horse camp or something. Long distance relationships are BS."

"But it would just be for the summer," I protested. "It's dumb to break up over a summer." I'd nursed a crush on Conrad for whole school years. I could survive for months, years, on a crush. It was like food. It could sustain me. If Conrad was mine, there was no way I'd break up with him over a summer—or a school year, for that matter.

Clay looked at me with his heavy-lidded, sleepy eyes and said, "Do you have a boyfriend?"

"Yes," I said, and I couldn't help myself—I looked at Conrad when I said it. *See,* I was saying, *I'm not a stupid twelve-year-old girl with a crush anymore. I'm a real person.* With an actual boyfriend. Who cared if it wasn't true? Conrad's eyes flickered, but his face was the same, expressionless. Jeremiah, though, he looked surprised.

"Belly, you have a boyfriend?" He frowned. "You never mentioned him."

"It's not that serious." I picked at an unraveling thread on the seat cushion. I was already regretting making it up. "In fact, we're really, really casual."

"See? Then what's the point of a relationship during summer? What if you meet people?" Clay winked at me in a jokey way. "Like right now?"

"We've already met, Clay. Like, ten years ago." Not that he'd ever actually paid me any attention.

He nudged me with his knee. "Nice to meet you. I'm Clay."

I laughed, even though it wasn't funny. It just felt like the right thing to do. "Hi, I'm Belly."

"So, Belly, are you gonna come to my bonfire tomorrow night?" he asked me.

"Um, sure," I said, trying not to sound too excited.

Conrad and Steven and Jeremiah went to the big Fourth of July bonfire every year. Clay had it at his house because there were a ton of fireworks on that end of the beach. His mom always put out stuff for s'mores. I once made Jeremiah bring one back for me, and he did. It was rubbery and burnt, but I still ate it, and I was still grateful to Jeremiah for it. It was like a little piece of the party. They never let me go with them, and I never tried to make them. I watched the show from our back porch, in my pajamas, with Susannah and my mother. They drank champagne and I drank Martinelli's Sparkling Cider.

"I thought you came down here to swim," Conrad said abruptly.

"Geez, give her a break, Con," Jeremiah said. "If she wants to swim, she'll swim."

We exchanged a look, our look that meant, *Why is Conrad such a freaking dad?* Conrad flicked his cigarette into his half-empty can. "Do what you want," he said.

"I will," I said, sticking my tongue out at Conrad and standing up. I threw off my towel and dove into the water, a perfect swan dive. I stayed underwater for a minute. Then I started doing the backstroke so I could eavesdrop on their conversation.

In a low voice I heard Clay say, "Man, Cousins is starting to get old. I want to hurry up and get back."

"Yeah, me too," Conrad said.

So Conrad was ready to leave. Even though a little

part of me knew that already, it still hurt. I wanted to say, Then leave already. If you don't want to be here, don't be here. Just leave. But I wasn't going to let Conrad bother me, not when things were finally looking up.

At last I was invited to Clay Bertolet's Fourth of July bonfire. I was one of the big kids now. Life was good. Or it was getting there, anyway.

I thought about what I was going to wear all day. Since I'd never been, I had no idea what to wear. Probably it would get cold, but who wanted to bundle up at a bonfire? Not for my first one. I also didn't want Conrad and Jeremiah to give me a hard time if I was too dressed up. I figured shorts, a tank top, and no shoes were the safe way to go.

When we got there, I saw that I had chosen wrong. The other girls were wearing sundresses and little skirts and Uggs. If I'd had girl friends at Cousins, I might have known that. "You didn't tell me that girls got dressed up," I hissed at Jeremiah.

"You look fine. Don't be dumb," he said, walking straight over to the keg. There was a keg. There were no graham crackers or marshmallows anywhere I could see.

I'd actually never seen a keg before in real life. Just in movies. I started to follow him, but Conrad grabbed my arm. "Don't drink tonight," he warned. "My mom will kill me if I let you drink."

I shook him off. "You're not 'letting' me do anything."

"Come on. Please?"

"We'll see," I said, walking away from him and toward the fire. I wasn't sure if I even wanted to drink. Even though I'd seen Clay drinking the night before, I'd still been expecting s'mores.

Going to the bonfire was nice in theory, but actually being there was something else. Jeremiah was chatting up some girl in a red, white, and blue bikini top and a jean skirt, and Conrad was talking to Clay and some other guys I didn't recognize. I thought after the way Clay had been flirty last night, he might at least come over to say hi. But he didn't. He had his hand on some girl's back.

I stood by the fire alone and pretended to warm my hands even though they weren't cold. That's when I saw him. He was standing alone too, drinking a bottle of water. It didn't seem like he knew anybody either, since he was standing all by himself. He looked like he was my age. But there was something about him that seemed safe and comfortable, like he was younger than me even though he wasn't. It took me a few glances to figure out what it was. When I finally figured it out, it was like, Aha!

It was his eyelashes. They were so long they practically hit his cheekbones. Granted, his cheekbones were high, but still. Also, he had a slight underbite, and his skin was clear and smooth, the color of toasted coconut flakes, the kind you put on ice cream. I touched my cheek and felt relieved that the sun had dried out the pimple from two days before. His skin was perfect. To my eyes, everything about him was pretty perfect.

He was tall, taller than Steven or Jeremiah, maybe even Conrad. He looked like he was maybe half-white, half-Japanese, or Korean maybe. He was so pretty I felt like I could draw his face, and I didn't even know how to draw.

He caught me looking at him, and I looked away. Then I looked back over and he caught me again. He raised his hand and waved it, just slightly.

I could feel my cheeks flaming. There was nothing for me to say but, "Hi." I walked over, stuck out my hand, and immediately regretted it. Who shook hands anymore?

He took my hand and shook it. He didn't say anything at first. He just stared at me, like he was trying to figure something out. "You look familiar," he said at last.

I tried not to smile. Wasn't that what boys said to girls when they came on to them at bars? I wondered if he'd seen me on the beach in my new polka-dot bikini. I'd only had the nerve to wear it the one time, but maybe that was what had gotten me noticed by this guy. "Maybe you've seen me on the beach?"

He shook his head. "No. . . . That's not it."

So it hadn't been the bikini, then. I tried again. "Maybe over at Scoops, the ice cream place?"

"No, that's not it either," he said. Then it was like the little light went on in his head, because he grinned suddenly. "Did you take Latin?"

What in the world? "Um . . . yes."

"Did you ever go to Latin Convention in Washington, DC?" he asked.

"Yes," I said. Who was this boy anyway?

He nodded, satisfied. "So did I. In eighth grade, right?"

"Yeah . . ." In eighth grade I had a retainer and I still wore glasses. I hated, hated that he knew me from back then. Why couldn't he know me from now, in my polka-dot bikini?

"That's how I know you. I've been standing here trying to figure it out." He grinned. "I'm Cam, but my Latin name was Sextus. Salve."

Suddenly giggles rose up in my chest like soda bubbles. It was kind of funny. "Salve. I'm Flavia. I mean, Belly. I mean, my name is Isabel, but everyone calls me Belly."

"Why?" He looked at me like he really wondered why.

"It's my dad's nickname for me from when I was little. He thought Isabel was too long a name," I explained. "Everyone just still calls me that. It's dumb."

He ignored the last part and said, "Why not Izzy, then? Or Belle?"

"I don't know. It's partly because Jelly Bellys are my

favorite, and my dad and I used to play this game. He'd ask me what kind of mood I was in, but I would answer him in Jelly Belly flavors. Like plum if I was in a good mood . . ." My voice trailed off. I babbled when I was nervous, and I was definitely nervous. I'd always hated the name Belly—partly because it wasn't even a real name. It was a child's nickname, not a real name at all. Isabel, on the other hand, was the name of an exotic kind of girl, the kind of girl who went to places like Morocco and Mozambique, who wore red nail polish year round and had dark bangs. Belly was the kind of name that conjured up images of plump children or men in wifebeaters. "Anyway, I hate the name Izzy, but I do wish people called me Belle. It's prettier."

He nodded. "That's what it means too. Beautiful."

"I know," I said. "I'm in AP French."

Cam said something in French, so fast I couldn't understand him.

"What?" I said. I felt stupid. It's embarrassing to speak French when it's not in a classroom. It's like, conjugating verbs is one thing, but actually speaking it, to an actual French person, is a whole different thing.

"My grandmother's French," he said. "I grew up speaking it."

"Oh." Now I felt stupid for bragging about being in AP French.

"You know, the *v* is supposed to be pronounced *w*."

"What?"

"In Flavia. It's supposed to be pronounced Fla-wia."

"Of course I know that," I snapped. "I took second prize in oration. But Flawia sounds dumb."

"I took first prize," he said, trying not to sound smug. I had a sudden memory of a boy in a black T-shirt and a striped tie, blowing everyone away with his Catullus speech, taking first place. It was him. "Why did you pick it if you thought it sounded dumb?"

I sighed. "Because Cornelia was taken. Everyone wanted to be Cornelia."

"Yeah, everyone wanted to be Sextus too."

"Why?" I said. Immediately I regretted it. "Oh. Never mind."

Cam laughed. "Eighth-grade boy humor isn't very developed."

I laughed too. Then I said, "So do you stay in a house around here?"

"We're renting the house two blocks down. My mom sort of made me come," Cam said, rubbing the top of his head self-consciously.

"Oh." I wished I would stop saying "oh," but I couldn't think of anything else.

"What about you? Why'd you come, Isabel?"

I was startled when he used my real name. It just rolled right off his tongue. It felt like the first day of school. But I liked it. "I don't know," I said. "I guess because Clay invited me."

Everything that came out of my mouth sounded so generic. For some reason I wanted to impress this boy. I wanted him to like me. I could feel him judging me, judging the dumb things I said. I'm smart too, I wanted to tell him. I told myself it was fine, it didn't matter if he thought I was smart or not. But it did.

"I think I'm going to leave soon," he said, finishing his water. He didn't look at me when he said, "Do you need a ride?"

"No," I said. I tried to swallow my disappointment that he was leaving already. "I came with those guys over there." I pointed at Conrad and Jeremiah.

He nodded. "I figured, the way your brother kept looking over here."

I almost choked. "My brother? Who? Him?" I pointed at Conrad. He wasn't looking at us. He was looking at a blond girl in a Red Sox cap, and she was looking right back. He was laughing, and he never laughed.

"Yeah."

"He's not my brother. He tries to act like he is, but he's not," I said. "He thinks he's everybody's big brother. It's so patronizing. . . . Why are you leaving already anyway? You're gonna miss the fireworks."

He cleared his throat like he was embarrassed. "Um, I was actually gonna go home and study."

"Latin?" I covered my mouth with my hand to keep from giggling.

"No. I'm studying whales. I want to intern on a whale watching boat, and I have to take this whaling exam next month," he said, rubbing the top of his head again.

"Oh. That's cool," I said. I wished he wasn't leaving already. I didn't want him to go. He was nice. Standing next to him, I felt like Thumbelina, little and precious. He was that tall. If he left, I'd be all alone. "You know what, maybe I will get a ride. Wait here. I'll be right back."

I hurried over to Conrad, walking so fast I kicked up sand behind me. "Hey, I'm gonna get a ride," I said breathlessly.

The blond Red Sox girl looked me up and down. "Hello," she said.

Conrad said, "With who?"

I pointed at Cam. "Him."

"You're not riding with someone you don't even know," he said flatly.

"I do so know him. He's Sextus."

He narrowed his eyes. "Sex what?"

"Never mind. His name is Cam, he's studying whales, and you don't get to decide who I ride home with. I was just letting you know, as a courtesy. I wasn't asking for your permission." I started to walk away, but he grabbed my elbow.

"I don't care what he's studying. It's not gonna happen," he said casually, but his grip was tight. "If you want to go, I'll take you."

I took a deep breath. I had to keep cool. I wasn't going to let him goad me into being a baby, not in front of all these people. "No, thanks," I said, trying to walk away again. But he didn't let go.

"I thought you already had a boyfriend?" His tone was mocking, and I knew he'd seen through my lie the night before.

I wanted so badly to throw a handful of sand in his face. I tried to twist out of his grip. "Let go of me! That hurts!"

He let go immediately, his face red. It didn't really hurt, but I wanted to embarrass him the way he was embarrassing me. I said loudly, "I'd rather ride with a stranger than with someone who's been drinking!"

"I've had one beer," he snapped. "I weigh a hundred and seventy-five pounds. Wait half an hour and I'll take you. Stop being such a brat."

I could feel tears starting to spark my eyelids. I looked over my shoulder to see if Cam was watching. He was. "You're an asshole," I said.

He looked me dead in the eyes and said, "And you're a four-year-old."

As I walked away, I heard the girl ask, "Is she your girlfriend?"

I whirled around, and we both said "No!" at the same time.

Confused, she said, "Well, is she your little sister?" like I wasn't standing right there. Her perfume was heavy. It felt like it filled all the air around us, like we were breathing her in.

"No, I'm not his little sister." I hated this girl for being a witness to all this. It was humiliating. And she was pretty, in the same kind of way Taylor was pretty, which somehow made things worse.

Conrad said, "Her mom is best friends with my mom." So that was all I was to him? His mom's friend's daughter?

I took a deep breath, and without even thinking, I said to the girl, "I've known Conrad my whole life. So let me be the one to tell you you're barking up the wrong tree. Conrad will never love anyone as much as he loves himself, if you know what I mean—" I lifted up my hand and wiggled my fingers.

"Shut up, Belly," Conrad warned. The tops of his ears were turning bright red. It was a low blow, but I didn't care. He deserved it.

Red Sox girl frowned. "What is she talking about, Conrad?"

To her I blurted out, "Oh, I'm sorry, do you not know what the idiom 'barking up the wrong tree' means?"

Her pretty face twisted. "You little skank," she hissed.

I could feel myself shrinking. I wished I could take it back. I'd never gotten into a fight with a girl before, or with anyone for that matter.

Thankfully, Conrad broke in then and pointed to the

bonfire. "Belly, go back over there, and wait for me to come get you," he said harshly.

That's when Jeremiah ambled over. "Hey, hey, what's going on?" he asked, smiling in his easy, goofy way.

"Your brother is a jerk," I said. "That's what's going on."

Jeremiah put his arm around me. He smelled like beer. "You guys play nice, you hear?"

I shrugged out of his hold and said, "I *am* playing nice. Tell your brother to play nice."

"Wait, are you guys brother and sister too?" the girl asked.

Conrad said, "Don't even think about leaving with that guy."

"Con, chill out," Jeremiah said. "She's not leaving. Right, Belly?"

He looked at me, and I pursed my lips and nodded. Then I gave Conrad the dirtiest look I could muster, and I shot one at the girl, too, when I was far enough away that she wouldn't be able to reach out and grab me by the hair. I walked back to the bonfire, trying to keep my shoulders straight and high, when inside I felt like a kid who'd gotten yelled at at her own birthday party. It wasn't fair, to be treated like I was a kid when I wasn't. I bet me and that girl were the same age.

Cam said, "What was that all about?"

I was choking back tears as I said, "Let's just go."

He hesitated, glancing back over at Conrad. "I don't think that's such a good idea, Flavia. But I'll stay here with you and hang out for a while. The whales can wait."

I wanted to kiss him then. I wanted to forget I ever knew Conrad and just be there, existing in the bubble of that moment. The first firework went off, somewhere high above us. It sounded like a teakettle whistling loud and proud. It was gold, and it exploded into millions of gold flecks, like confetti over our heads.

We sat by the fire and he told me about whales and I told him about stupid things, like being secretary of French Club, and how my favorite food was pulled pork sandwiches. He said he was a vegetarian. We must have sat there for an hour. I could feel Conrad watching us the whole time, and I was so tempted to give him the finger—I hated it when he won.

When it started to get cold, I rubbed my arms, and Cam took off his hoodie and gave it to me. Which, was sort of my dream come true—getting cold and having a guy actually give you his hoodie instead of gloating over how smart he'd been to bring one.

Underneath, his T-shirt said STRAIGHT EDGE, with a picture of a razor blade, the kind a guy shaves with. "What does that mean?" I asked, zipping up his hoodie. It was warm and it smelled like boy, but in a good way.

"I'm straight edge," he said. "I don't drink or do drugs. I used to be hardcore, where you don't take over-the-counter medicine or drink caffeine, but I quit that."

"Why?"

"Why was I hardcore straight edge or why did I quit?"

"Both."

"I don't believe in polluting your body with unnatural stuff," he said. "I quit because it was making my mom crazy. And I also just really missed Dr Pepper."

I liked Dr Pepper too. I was glad I hadn't been drinking. I didn't want him to think badly of me. I wanted him to think I was cool, like the kind of girl who didn't care what people thought, the kind of person he obviously was. I wanted to be his friend. I also wanted to kiss him.

Cam left when we left. He got up as soon as he saw Jeremiah coming over to get me. "So long, Flavia," he said.

I started to unzip his hoodie, and he said, "That's all right. You can give it to me later."

"Here, I'll give you my number," I said, holding my hand out for his phone. I'd never given a boy my phone number before. As I punched in my number, I felt really proud of myself for offering it to him.

Backing away, he put the phone into his pocket and said, "I would have found a way to get it back without your number. I'm smart, remember? First prize in oration."

I tried not to smile as he walked away. "You're not that smart," I called out. It felt like fate that we'd met. It felt like the most romantic thing that had ever happened to me, and it was.

I watched Conrad say good-bye to Red Sox girl. She gave him a hug, and he hugged her back, but not really. I was glad I had ruined his night, if only a little bit.

On the way to the car a girl stopped me. She wore her blondish-brown hair in two pigtails, and she had on a pink low-cut shirt. "Do you like Cam?" the girl asked me casually. I wondered how she knew him—I thought he'd been a nobody just like me.

"I barely even know him," I told her, and her face relaxed. She was relieved. I recognized that look in her eyes—dreamy and hopeful. It must have been the way I looked when I used to talk about Conrad, used to try to think of ways to insert his name into conversation. It made me sad for her, for me.

"I saw the way Nicole talked to you," she said abruptly. "Don't worry about her. She sucks as a person."

"Red Sox girl? Yeah, she kind of does suck at being a person," I agreed. Then I waved good-bye to her as Jeremiah and Conrad and I made our way to the car.

Conrad drove. He was completely sober, and I knew he had been all along. He checked out Cam's hoodie, but he didn't say anything. We didn't speak to each other once. Jeremiah and I both sat in the backseat, and he tried to joke around, but nobody laughed. I was too busy thinking, remembering everything that had happened that night. I thought to myself, *That might have been the best night of my life.*

In my yearbook the year before, Sean Kirkpatrick wrote that I had "eyes so clear" he could "see right into my soul." Sean was a drama geek, but so what. It still made me feel good. Taylor snickered when I showed it to her. She said only Sean Kirkpatrick would notice the color of my eyes when the rest of the guys were too busy looking at my chest. But this wasn't Sean Kirkpatrick. This was Cam, a real guy who had noticed me even before I was pretty.

I was brushing my teeth in the upstairs bathroom when Jeremiah came in, shutting the door behind him. Reaching for his toothbrush, he said, "What's going on with you and Con? Why are you guys so mad at each other?" He hopped up onto the sink.

Jeremiah hated it when people fought. It was part of why he always played the clown. He took it upon himself to bring levity to any situation. It was sweet but also kind of annoying.

Through a mouthful of toothpaste I said, "Um, because he's a self-righteous neo-maxi-zoom-dweebie?"

We both laughed at that. It was one of our little inside jokes, a line from *The Breakfast Club* that we spent repeating to each other the summer I was eight and he was nine.

He cleared his throat. "Seriously, though, don't be so hard on him. He's going through some stuff."

This was news to me. "What? What stuff?" I demanded.

Jeremiah hesitated. "It's not up to me to tell you."

"Come on. We tell each other everything, Jere. No secrets, remember?"

He smiled. "I remember. But I still can't tell you. It's not my secret."

Frowning, I turned the faucet on and said, "You always take his side."

"I'm not taking his side. I'm just telling his side."

"Same thing."

He reached out and turned the corners of my mouth up. It was one of his oldest tricks; no matter what, it made me smile. "No pouting, Bells, remember?"

No Pouting was a rule Conrad and Steven had made up one summer. I think I was eight or nine. The thing was, it only applied to me. They even put a sign up on my bedroom door. I tore it down, of course, and I ran and told Susannah and my mother. That night I got seconds on dessert, I remember. Anytime I acted the slightest bit sad or unhappy, one of the boys would start yelling, "No pouting. No pouting." And, okay, maybe I did pout a lot, but it was the only way I could ever get my way. In some ways it was even harder being the only girl back then. In some ways not.

chapter *twenty-two*

That night I slept in Cam's hoodie. It was stupid and kind of sappy, but I didn't care. And the next day I wore it outside, even though it was blazing hot out. I loved how the sleeves were frayed, the way it felt lived in. It felt like a boy's.

Cam was the first boy to pay attention to me like that, to be up front about the fact that he actually wanted to hang out with me. And not be, like, embarrassed about it.

When I woke up, I realized that I had given him the house number. I didn't know why. I could have given him my cell phone number just as easily.

I kept waiting for the phone to ring. The phone never rang at the summer house. The only people who called the house phone were Susannah, trying to figure out what kind of fish we wanted for dinner, or my mother, calling to tell Steven to put the towels in the dryer, or to get the grill going.

I stayed on the deck, sunning and reading magazines with Cam's hoodie balled up in my lap like a stuffed animal. Since we kept the windows open, I knew I'd hear if the phone rang.

I slathered myself with sunscreen first, and then two layers of tanning oil. I didn't know if it was an oxymoron or what, but better safe than sorry was how I figured it. I set myself up with a little station of cherry Kool-Aid in an old water bottle, plus a radio, plus sunglasses, and magazines. The sunglasses were a pair that Susannah had bought me years ago. Susannah loved to buy presents. When she went off for errands, she'd come home with presents. Little things, like this pair of red heart sunglasses she said I just had to have. She knew just what I'd love, things I hadn't even thought of, had certainly never thought of buying. Things like lavender foot lotion, or a silk quilted pouch for tissues.

My mother and Susannah had left early that morning for one of their art gallery trips to Dyerstown, and Conrad, thank God, had left for work already. Jeremiah was still asleep. The house was mine.

The idea of tanning sounds so fun in theory. Laying out, soaking up sun and sipping on soda, falling asleep like a fat cat. But then the actual act of it is kind of tedious and boring. And hot. I would always rather be floating in an ocean, catching sun that way, than lying down sweating in the sun. They say you get tanner faster when you're wet, anyhow.

But that morning I had no choice. In case Cam called, I mean. So I lay there, sweating and sizzling like a piece of chicken on a grill. It was boring, but it was a necessity.

Just after ten, the phone rang. I sprang up and ran into the kitchen. "Hello?" I said breathlessly.

"Hi, Belly. It's Mr. Fisher."

"Oh, hi, Mr. Fisher," I said. I tried not to sound too disappointed.

He cleared his throat. "So, how's it going down there?"

"Pretty good. Susannah's not home, though. She and my mom went to Dyerstown to visit some galleries."

"I see. . . . How are the boys?"

"Good . . ." I never knew what to say to Mr. Fisher. "Conrad's at work and Jeremiah's still asleep. Do you want me to wake him up?"

"No, no, that's all right."

There was this long pause, and I scrambled to think of something to say.

"Are you, um, coming down this weekend?" I asked.

"No, not this weekend," he said. His voice sounded really far away. "I'll just call back later. You have fun, Belly."

I hung up the phone. Mr. Fisher hadn't been down to Cousins once yet. He used to come the weekend after the Fourth, because it was easier getting away from work after the holiday. When he came, he'd fire up the barbecue all weekend long, and he'd wear his apron that said CHEF KNOWS BEST. I wondered if Susannah would be sad he wasn't coming, if the boys would care.

I trudged back to my lounge chair, back to the sun. I fell asleep on my lounge chair, and I woke up to Jeremiah sprinkling Kool-Aid onto my stomach. "Quit it," I said grouchily, sitting up. I was thirsty from my extra sweet Kool-Aid (I always made it with double sugar), and I felt dehydrated and sweaty.

He laughed and sat down on my lounge chair. "Is this what you're doing all day?"

"Yes," I said, wiping off my stomach and then wiping my hand on his shorts.

"Don't be boring. Come do something with me," he ordered. "I don't have to work until tonight."

"I'm working on my tan," I told him.

"You're tan enough."

"Will you let me drive?"

He hesitated. "Fine," he said. "But you have to rinse off first. I don't want you getting my seat all oily."

I stood up, throwing my limp greasy hair into a high ponytail. "I'll go right now. Just wait," I said.

Jeremiah waited for me in the car, with the AC on full

blast. He sat in the passenger seat. "Where are we going?" I asked, getting into the driver's seat. I felt like an old pro. "Tennessee? New Mexico? We have to go far so I can get good practice."

He closed his eyes and laid his head back. "Just take a left out of the driveway," he told me.

"Yessir," I said, turning off the AC and opening all four windows. It was so much better driving with the windows down. It felt like you were actually going somewhere.

He continued giving me directions, and then we pulled up to Go Kart City. "Are you serious?"

"We're gonna get you some driving practice," he said, grinning like crazy.

We waited in line for the cars, and when it was our turn, the guy told me to get in the blue one. I said, "Can I drive the red one instead?"

He winked at me and said, "You're so pretty, I'd let you drive *my* car."

I could feel myself blush, but I liked it. The guy was older than me, and he was actually paying me attention. It was kind of amazing. I'd seen him there the summer before, and he hadn't looked at me once.

Getting into the car next to me, Jeremiah muttered, "What a freaking cheeseball. He needs to get a real job."

"Like lifeguarding is a real job?" I countered.

Jeremiah scowled. "Just drive."

Every time my car came back around the track, the guy waved at me. The third time he did it, I waved back.

We rode around the track a bunch of times, until it was time for Jeremiah to go to work.

"I think you've had enough driving for today," Jeremiah said, rubbing his neck. "I'll drive us home."

I didn't argue with him. He drove home fast, and dropped me off at the curb and headed to work. I stepped back into the house feeling very tired and tan. And also satisfied.

"Someone named Cam called for you," my mother said. She was sitting at the kitchen table, reading the paper with her horn-rimmed reading glasses on. She didn't look up.

"He did?" I asked, covering my smile with the back of my hand. "Well, did he leave a number?"

"No," she said. "He said he'd call back."

"Why didn't you ask for it?" I said, and I hated the whininess in my voice, but when it came to my mother, it was like I couldn't help it.

That's when she looked at me, perplexed. "I don't know. He wasn't offering it. Who is he anyway?"

"Forget it," I told her, walking over to the refrigerator for some lemonade.

"Suit yourself," my mother said, going back to her paper.

She didn't press the issue. She never did. She at least could have gotten his number. If Susannah had been down here instead of her, she would have been singsongy and she would have teased and snooped until I told her everything. Which I would have, gladly.

"Mr. Fisher called this morning," I said.

My mother looked up again. "What did he say?"

"Nothing much. Just that he can't come this weekend."

She pursed her lips, but she didn't say anything.

"Where's Susannah?" I asked. "Is she in her room?"

"Yes, but she doesn't feel well. She's taking a nap," my mother said. In other words, Don't go up and bother her.

"What's wrong with her?"

"She has a summer cold," my mother said automatically.

My mother was a terrible liar. Susannah had been spending a lot of time in her room, and there was a sadness to her that hadn't been there before. I knew something was up. I just wasn't completely sure what.

chapter *twenty-three*

Cam called again the next night, and the night after that. We talked on the phone twice before we met up again, for, like, four or five hours at a time. When we talked, I lay on one of the lounge chairs on the porch and stared up at the moon with my toes pointed toward the sky. I laughed so hard that Jeremiah yelled out his window for me to keep it down. We talked about everything, and I loved it, but the whole time I wondered when he was going to ask to see me again. He didn't.

So I had to take matters into my own hands. I invited Cam to come over and play video games and maybe swim. I felt like some kind of liberated woman calling him up and inviting him over, like it was the kind of thing I did all the time. When really, I was only doing it because I knew no one was going to be at home. I didn't want Jeremiah or Conrad or my mother or even Susannah to see him just yet. For now, he was just mine.

"I'm a really good swimmer, so don't be mad when we race and I beat you," I said over the phone.

He laughed and said, "At freestyle?"

"At any style."

"Why do you like to win so much?"

I didn't have an answer for that, except to say that winning was fun, and anyway, who didn't like to win? Growing up with Steven and spending my summers with Jeremiah and Conrad, winning was always important, and doubly so because I was a girl and was never expected to win anything. Victory is a thousand times sweeter when you're the underdog.

Cam came over, and I watched from my bedroom window as he drove up. His car was navy blue and old and beat-up looking, like his hoodie that I was already planning on keeping. It looked like exactly the kind of car he'd drive.

He rang the doorbell, and I flew down the stairs to open the door. "Hi," I said. I was wearing his hoodie.

"You're wearing my hoodie," he said, smiling down at me. He was even taller than I'd remembered.

"You know, I was thinking that I want to keep it," I told him, letting him in and closing the door behind me. "But I don't expect to get it for free. I'll race you for it."

"But if we race, you can't be mad if I beat you," he

said, raising an eyebrow at me. "It's my favorite hoodie, and if I win, I'm taking it."

"No problem," I told him.

We went out to the pool through the back screen door, down the porch steps. I threw off my shorts and T-shirt and his hoodie quickly, without even thinking—Jeremiah and I raced all the time in the pool. It didn't occur to me to be self-conscious to be in a bikini in front of Cam. After all, we spent the whole summer in bathing suits in that house.

But he looked away quickly and took off his T-shirt. "Ready?" he said, standing by the edge.

I walked over next to him. "One full lap?" I asked, dipping my toe into the water.

"Sure," he said. "You want a head start?"

I snorted. "Do *you* want a head start?"

"Touché," he said, grinning.

I'd never heard a boy say "touché" before. Or anyone else, for that matter. Maybe my mother. But on him it looked good. It was different.

I won the first race easily. "You let me win," I accused.

"No, I didn't," he said, but I knew it wasn't true. In all the summers and all of the races, no boy, not Conrad or Jeremiah or certainly not Steven, had ever let me win.

"You better give it your all this time," I warned. "Or I'm keeping the hoodie."

"Best two out of three," Cam said, wiping the hair out of his eyes.

He won the next heat, and I won the last one. I wasn't fully convinced that he didn't just let me win—after all, he was so tall and long, his one stroke was worth two of mine. But I wanted to keep the hoodie, so I didn't challenge the win. After all, a win was a win.

When he had to leave, I walked him to his car. He didn't get in right away. There was this long pause, the first we'd had, if you can believe it. Cam cleared his throat and said, "So this guy I know, Kinsey, is having a party tomorrow night. Do you maybe want to come?"

"Yeah," I said right away. "I do."

I made the mistake of mentioning it at breakfast the next morning. My mother and Susannah were grocery shopping. It was just me and the boys, the way it had been for the most part this summer. "I'm going to a party tonight," I said, partly just to say it out loud and partly to brag.

Conrad raised his eyebrows. "You?"

"Whose party?" Jeremiah demanded. "Kinsey's?"

I put down my juice. "How'd you know?"

Jeremiah laughed and wagged his finger at me. "I know everybody in Cousins, Belly. I'm a lifeguard. That's like being the mayor. Greg Kinsey works at that surf shop over by the mall."

Frowning, Conrad said, "Doesn't Greg Kinsey sell crystal meth out of his trunk?"

"What? No. Cam wouldn't be friends with someone like that," I said defensively.

"Who's Cam?" Jeremiah asked me.

"That guy I met at Clay's bonfire. He asked me to go to this party with him, and I said yes."

"Sorry. You aren't going to some meth addict's party," Conrad said.

This was the second time Conrad was trying to tell me what to do, and I was sick of it. Who did he think he was? I had to go to this party. I didn't care if there was crystal meth or not, I was going. "I'm telling you, Cam wouldn't be friends with someone like that! He's straight edge."

Conrad and Jeremiah both snorted. In moments like these, they were a team. "He's straight edge?" Jeremiah said, trying not to smile. "Neat."

"Very cool," agreed Conrad.

I glared at the both of them. First they didn't want me hanging out with meth addicts, and then being straight edge wasn't cool either. "He doesn't do drugs, all right? Which is why I highly doubt he'd be friends with a drug dealer."

Jeremiah scratched his cheek and said, "You know what, it might be Greg Rosenberg who's the meth dealer. Greg Kinsey's pretty cool. He has a pool table. I think I'll check this party out too."

"Wait, what?" I was starting to panic.

"I think I'll go too," Conrad said. "I like pool."

I stood up. "You guys can't come. You weren't invited."

Conrad leaned back in his chair and put his arms behind his head. "Don't worry, Belly. We won't bother you on your big date."

"Unless he puts his hands on you." Jeremiah ground his fist into his hand threateningly, his blue eyes narrow. "Then his ass is grass."

"This isn't happening," I moaned. "You guys, I'm begging you. Don't come. Please, please don't come."

Jeremiah ignored me. "Con, what are you gonna wear?"

"I haven't thought about it. Maybe my khaki shorts? What are *you* gonna wear?"

"I hate you guys," I said.

Things had been weird with me and Conrad and also with me and Jeremiah—an impossible thought crept its way into my head. Was it possible they didn't want me with Cam? Because *they*, like, had feelings for me? Could that even be? I doubted it. I was like a little sister to them. Only, I wasn't.

When I finished getting ready and it was almost time to go, I stopped by Susannah's room to say good-bye. She and my mother were holed up in there sorting through old pictures. Susannah was all ready for bed, even though it was still pretty early. She had her pillows propped up around her, and she was wearing one of her silk robes that Mr. Fisher had bought her on a business trip to Hong Kong. It was poppy and cream, and when I got married, I wanted one just like it.

"Come sit down and help us put this album together," my mother said, rifling through an old striped hatbox.

"Laurel, can't you see she's all dressed up? She's got better things to do than look at dusty old pictures." Susannah winked at me. "Belly, you look fresh as a daisy. I love you in white with your tan. It sets you off like a picture frame."

"Thanks, Susannah," I said.

I wasn't all that dressed up, but I wasn't in shorts like the night of the bonfire. I was wearing a white sundress and flip-flops, and I'd put my hair in braids while it was still wet. I knew I'd probably take them out in about half an hour because they were so tight, but I didn't care. They were cute.

"You do look lovely. Where are you headed?" my mother asked me.

"Just to a party," I said.

My mother frowned and said, "Are Conrad and Jeremiah going to this party too?"

"They're not my bodyguards," I said, rolling my eyes.

"I didn't say they were," my mother said.

Susannah waved me off and said, "Have fun, Belly!"

"I will," I said, shutting the door before my mother could ask me any more questions.

I'd hoped that Conrad and Jeremiah had just been kidding around, that they weren't really gonna try to come. But when I ran down the stairs to meet Cam's car, Jeremiah called out, "Hey, Belly?"

He and Conrad were watching TV in the family room. I poked my head in the doorway. "What?" I snapped. "I'm kind of in a hurry."

Jeremiah turned his head toward me and winked lazily. "See you soon."

Conrad looked at me and said, "What's with the perfume? It's giving me a headache. And why are you wearing all that makeup?"

I wasn't wearing that much makeup. I had some blush and mascara and a little lip gloss, that was it. It was just that he wasn't used to me wearing any. And I'd sprayed my neck and wrists, that was all. Conrad sure hadn't minded Red Sox girl's perfume. He'd loved *her* perfume. Still, I took one last look at myself in the mirror in the hallway—and I rubbed a little of the blush off, also the perfume.

Then I slammed the door shut and ran down the driveway, where Cam was turning in. I'd been watching from my bedroom window so I'd know the exact moment he drove up, so he wouldn't have to come inside and meet my mother.

I hopped into Cam's car. "Hi," I said.

"Hi. I would've rung the doorbell," he told me.

"Trust me, it's better this way," I said, suddenly feeling very shy. How is it possible to talk to someone on the phone for hours and hours, to even swim with this person, and then feel like you don't know them?

"So this guy Kinsey, he's kind of weird, but he's a good person," Cam told me as he backed out of the driveway. He was a good driver, careful.

Casually I asked, "Does he by any chance sell crystal meth?"

"Um, not that I know of," he told me, smiling. His right cheek had a dimple in it that I hadn't noticed the other night. It was nice.

I relaxed. Now that the crystal meth stuff was out of the way, there was only one more thing. I twisted the charm bracelet on my wrist over and over and said, "So, you know those guys I was with at the bonfire? Jeremiah and Conrad?"

"Your fake brothers?"

"Yeah. I think they might be stopping by the party too. They know, um, Kinsey," I said.

"Oh, really?" he said. "Cool. Maybe they'll see that I'm not some kind of creep."

"They don't think you're a creep," I told him. "Well, they kind of do, but they'd think any guy I talk to is a creep, so it's nothing personal."

"They must really care about you a lot to be so protective," he said.

Did they?

"Um, not really. Well, Jeremiah does, but Conrad is all about duty. Or he used to be anyway. He should've been one of those samurais." I glanced over at him. "I'm sorry. Is this boring?"

"No, keep talking," Cam said. "How do you know about samurais?"

Tucking my legs under my butt, I said, "Ms. Baskerville's global studies class in ninth grade. We did a whole unit on Japan and Bushido. I was, like, obsessed with the idea of seppuku."

"My dad's half-Japanese," he said. "My grandmother lives there, so we go out and visit her once a year."

"Wow." I'd never been to Japan, or anywhere in Asia for that matter. My mother's travels hadn't taken her there yet either, though I knew she wanted to go. "Do you speak Japanese?"

"A little," he said, rubbing the top of his head. "I get by okay."

I whistled—my whistle was something I was proud of. My brother, Steven, had taught me. "So you speak English, French, and Japanese? That's pretty amazing. You're like some kind of genius, huh," I teased.

"I speak Latin, too," he reminded me, grinning.

"Latin's not spoken. It's a dead language," I said, just to be contrary.

"It's not dead. It's in every Western language." He sounded like my seventh-grade Latin teacher, Mr. Coney.

When we pulled up to this guy Kinsey's house, I kind of didn't want to get out of the car. I loved the feeling of talking and having somebody really listen to what I had to say. It was like a high or something. In this weird way, I felt powerful.

We parked in the cul-de-sac—there were a ton of cars. Some were halfway on the lawn. Cam walked quickly. His legs were so long that I had to hurry to keep up. "So how do you know this guy?" I asked him.

"He's my supplier." He laughed at the expression on my face. "You're really gullible, Flavia. His parents have a boat. I've seen him down at the marina. He's a nice guy."

We walked right in without knocking. The music was so loud I could hear it from the driveway. It was karaoke music—there was a girl singing "Like a Virgin" at the top of her lungs and rolling around on the ground, her mike getting twisted up in her jeans. There were ten or so people in the living room, drinking beer and passing around a songbook. "Sing 'Livin' on a Prayer' next," some guy urged the girl on the floor.

A couple of guys I didn't recognize were checking me out—I could feel their eyes on me, and I wondered if I really had worn too much makeup. It was a new thing to have guys looking at me, much less asking me on dates. It felt equal parts amazing and scary. I spotted the girl from the bonfire, the one who liked Cam. She looked at us, and then she looked away, sneaking glances every once in a while. I felt bad for her; I knew how that felt.

I also recognized our neighbor Jill, who spent weekends at Cousins—she waved at me, and it occurred to me that I'd never seen her outside of the neighborhood, our front yards. She was sitting next to the guy from the video store, the one who worked on Tuesdays and wore his name tag upside down. I'd never seen the lower half of his body before, he was always standing behind the counter. And then there was the waitress Katie from Jimmy's Crab Shack without her red-and-white striped uniform. These were people I'd been seeing every summer for my whole life. So this is where they'd been all this time. Out, at parties, while I'd been left out, locked away in the summer house like Rapunzel, watching old movies with my mother and Susannah.

Cam seemed to know everybody. He said hi, shoulder-bumping guys and hugging girls. He introduced me. He called me his friend Flavia. "Meet my friend Flavia," he said. "This is Kinsey. This is his house."

"Hi, Kinsey," I said.

Kinsey was sprawled out on the couch, and he wasn't wearing a shirt. He had a scrawny bird chest. He didn't look like a meth dealer. He looked like a paperboy.

He took a gulp of beer and said, "My name's not really Kinsey. It's Greg. Everybody just calls me Kinsey."

"My name's not really Flavia. It's Belly. Only Cam calls me Flavia."

Kinsey nodded like that actually made sense. "You guys want something to drink, there's a cooler in the kitchen."

Cam said, "Do you want something to drink?"

I wasn't sure if I should say yes or not. On the one hand, yeah, I kind of did. I never drank. It would be, like, an experience. Further proof that this summer was special, important. On the other hand, would he be grossed out by me if I did? Would he judge me for it? I didn't know what the straight edge rules were.

I decided against it. The last thing I needed was to smell like Clay had the other night. "I'll have a Coke," I told him.

Cam nodded, and I could tell he approved. We headed over to the kitchen. As we walked, I heard little snatches of conversation—"I heard Kelly got a DUI and that's why she isn't here this summer." "I heard she got kicked out of school." I wondered who Kelly was. I wondered if I'd recognize her if I saw her. It was all Steven and Jeremiah and Conrad's fault—they never took me anywhere. That was why I didn't know anybody.

All of the chairs in the kitchen had purses and jackets

on them, so Cam moved over some empty beer bottles and made an empty space on the counter. I hopped up and sat on it.

"Do you know all these people?" I asked Cam.

"Not really," he said. "I just wanted you to think I was cool."

"I already do," I said, and I blushed almost immediately.

He laughed like I had made a joke, which made me feel better. He opened up the cooler and pulled out a Coke. He opened it and handed it to me.

Cam said, "Just because I'm straight edge doesn't mean you can't drink. I mean, I'll judge you for it, but you can still drink if you want to. That was a joke, by the way."

"I know," I said. "But I'm good with this Coke." Which was true.

I took a long sip of my Coke and burped. "Scuse me," I said, unraveling one of my braids. They were already too tight, and my head felt sore.

"You burp, like, baby burps," he said. "It's kind of gross but also kind of cute."

I unraveled the other braid and hit him on the shoulder. In my head I heard Conrad go, *Ooh, you're hitting him now. Way to flirt, Belly, way to flirt.* Even when he wasn't there, he was there. And then he really was.

Out of nowhere, I heard Jeremiah's signature yodel on the karaoke machine. I bit my lip. "They're here," I said.

"You want to go out and say hi?"

"Not really," I said, but I hopped down from the counter.

We went back to the living room, and Jeremiah was center stage, falsetto and singing some song I'd never heard of. The girls were laughing and watching him, all googly-eyed. And Conrad, he was on the couch with a beer in his hand. Red Sox girl was perched on the armrest next to him, leaning in close and letting her hair fall in his face like a curtain that encased the two of them. I wondered if they'd picked her up, if he'd let her sit shotgun.

"He's a good singer," Cam said. Then he looked where I was looking and said, "Are he and Nicole together?"

"Who knows?" I said. "Who cares?"

Jeremiah spotted me then, as he bowed at the end of his song. "Belly! This next song goes out to you." He pointed at Cam. "What's your name?"

Cam cleared his throat. "Cam. Cameron."

Jeremiah said right into the mike, "Your name is Cam Cameron? Damn, that sucks, dude." Everyone laughed, especially Conrad, when just a second ago he'd looked so bored.

"It's just Cam," Cam said quietly. He looked at me then, and I was embarrassed. Not for him, but of him. I hated them for that.

It was like Conrad and Jeremiah had deemed him

unworthy and so I had to too. It was funny how I'd felt so close to him just a few minutes before.

"Okay, Cam Cameron. This song goes out to you and our favorite little Belly Button. Hit it, ladies." Some girl pushed the play button on the remote. "Summer lovin', had me a blast . . ."

I wanted to kill him, but all I could do was shake my head at him and glare. It wasn't like I could grab the mike out of his hand in front of all these people. Jeremiah just grinned at me and started to dance. One of the girls sitting on the floor jumped up and started dancing with him. She sang the Olivia Newton-John part, off-key. Conrad watched in his amused, condescending way. I heard someone say, "Who is that girl anyway?" She was looking right at me as she said it.

Next to me, Cam was laughing. I couldn't believe it. I was dying of embarrassment and he was laughing. "Smile, Flavia," he said, poking me in the side.

When someone tells me to smile, I can't help it. I always do.

Midway through Jeremiah's song, Cam and I walked out—without even looking, I knew Conrad was watching us.

Cam and I sat on the staircase and talked. He sat on the step above me. He was nice to talk to, not intimidating at all. I loved the way he laughed so easily—not like with Conrad. With Conrad you had to work hard for every smile. Nothing ever came easy with Conrad.

The way Cam was leaning into me, I thought he might try to kiss me. I was pretty sure I'd let him. But he'd lean in and scratch his ankle, or tug at his sock, and then shift away, and then he'd do it again.

When he was in the middle of a lean in, I heard pissed off, belligerent voices coming from the deck outside. One of them was definitely Conrad's pissed off, belligerent voice. I jumped up. "Something's going on out there."

"Let's check it out," said Cam, leading the way.

Conrad and some guy with a barbed wire tattoo on his forearm were arguing. The guy was shorter than Conrad, but stockier. He was packing some serious muscle, and he looked like he was, like, twenty-five. Jeremiah watched, bemused, but I could tell he was alert, ready to jump in if he needed to.

To Jeremiah I whispered, "What are they fighting about?"

He shrugged. "Conrad's wasted. Don't worry about it. They're just showing off."

"They look like they might kill each other," I said uneasily.

"They're fine," Cam said. "But we should probably get out of here. It's late."

I glanced at him. I'd almost forgotten he was standing next to me. "I'm not leaving," I said. Not that I could do anything to stop a fight from happening. But it wouldn't be right to just leave him there.

Conrad stepped up close to the tattoo guy, who

shoved him away easily, and Conrad laughed. I could feel an actual fight brewing, like a thunderstorm. Just like the way the water got really still before the sky broke open.

"Are you gonna do something?" I hissed.

"He's a big boy," Jeremiah said, his eyes close on Conrad. "He'll be fine."

But he didn't believe it, and neither did I. Conrad didn't seem fine at all. He didn't seem like the Conrad Fisher I knew, all wild and out of control. What if he got himself hurt? What then? I had to help, I just had to.

I started walking over to them, and I waved off Jeremiah when he tried to stop me. When I got there, I realized I had no idea what to say. I had never tried to break up a fight before.

"Um, hi," I said, standing between the two of them. "We have to leave."

Conrad pushed me out of the way. "Get the hell out of here, Belly."

"Who is this? Your baby sister?" The guy looked me up and down.

"No. I'm Belly," I told him. Only, I was nervous, and I stuttered when I said my name.

"Belly?" The guy busted out laughing, and I grabbed Conrad's arm.

"We're gonna leave now," I said.

I realized how drunk he was when he swayed a little as he tried to swat me off. "Don't leave. Things are just getting fun. See, I'm about to kick this guy's ass." I'd never seen him like this before. His intensity scared me. I wondered where Red Sox girl had gone. I kind of wished she was here to handle Conrad and not me. I didn't know what I was supposed to do.

The guy laughed, but I could tell he wanted a fight just about as much as I did. He looked tired, like all he wanted was to head home and watch TV in his boxers. Whereas Conrad was running on all cylinders. Conrad was like a soda bottle that had been shaken up; he was about to explode on somebody. It didn't matter who it was. It didn't matter that this guy was bigger than him. It wouldn't have mattered if he was twenty feet tall and built like a brick. Conrad was looking for a fight. He wouldn't be satisfied until he got one. And this guy, he could kill Conrad.

The guy kept looking at Conrad and then back at me. Shaking his head, he said, "Belly, you better get this little boy home."

"Don't talk to her," Conrad warned.

I put my hand on Conrad's chest. I had never done that before. It felt solid and warm; I could feel his heart beating fast and out of control. "Can we please just go home," I pleaded. But it was like Conrad didn't even see me standing there, or feel my hand on his chest.

"Listen to your girlfriend, kid," the guy said.

"I'm not his girlfriend," I said, glancing over at Cam, who had no expression on his face.

Then I looked back at Jeremiah helplessly, and he ambled over. He whispered something in Conrad's ear, and Conrad shook him off. But Jeremiah kept talking to him in his low voice, and when they looked at me, I realized it was about me. Conrad hesitated, and then he finally nodded. Then he half jokingly made like he was going to hit the guy, and the guy rolled his eyes. "Good night, douche," he said to the guy.

The guy waved him off with one hand. I let out a big breath.

As we walked back to the car, Cam grabbed my arm. "Are you okay to go home with these guys?" he asked me.

Conrad whirled around and said, "Who is this guy?"

I shook my head at Cam and said, "I'll be fine. Don't worry. I'll call you."

He looked worried. "Who's driving?"

"I am," Jeremiah said, and Conrad didn't argue. "Don't worry, Straight Edge, I don't drink and drive."

I was embarrassed, and I could tell Cam was bothered, but he just nodded. Quickly I hugged him, and he felt stiff. I wanted to make things okay. "Thanks for tonight," I said.

I watched him walk away, and I felt a stab of resentment—Conrad and his stupid temper had ruined my first real date. It wasn't fair.

Jeremiah said, "You guys get in the car; I left my hat inside. I'll be right back."

"Just hurry," I told him.

Conrad and I got in the car silently. It felt eerily quiet, and even though it was only just past one, it felt like it was four in the morning and the whole world had gone to sleep. He lay down in the backseat, all of his energy from before gone. I sat in the front seat with my bare feet on the dashboard, leaning back far in the seat. Neither of us spoke. It had been frightening back there. I didn't recognize him, the way he'd acted. I suddenly felt very tired.

My hair was hanging low, and from the backseat, all of a sudden, I felt Conrad touching it, running his fingers through the bottom. I think I stopped breathing. We were sitting in perfect silence, and Conrad Fisher was playing with my hair.

"Your hair is like a little kid's, the way it's always so messy," he said softly. His voice made me shiver, it was like the sound of water when it pulls off the sand.

I didn't say anything. I didn't even look at him. I didn't want to scare him off. It was like the time I had a really high fever, and everything felt gauzy and dizzy and unreal, it felt just like that. All I knew was, I didn't want him to stop.

But he finally did. I watched him in the visor mirror. He closed his eyes and sighed. I did too.

"Belly," he began.

Just as suddenly, everything in me was alert. The sleepy feeling was gone; every part of my body was awake now. I was holding my breath, waiting for what he would say. I didn't answer him. I didn't want to break the spell.

That's when Jeremiah came back, opened the door, slammed it shut. This moment between us, fragile and tenuous, snapped in half. It was over. It would do no good to wonder what he was going to say. Moments, when lost, can't be found again. They're just gone.

Jeremiah looked at me funny. I could tell he knew that he'd walked in on something. I shrugged at him, and he turned away and started the car.

I reached over to the radio and turned it on, loud.

The whole way home, there was this strange tension, everyone keeping quiet—Conrad passed out in the backseat, Jeremiah and me not looking at each other in the front seat. Until we pulled up the driveway, when Jeremiah said to Conrad, in what was a harsh tone for him, "Don't let Mom see you like this."

Which was when I realized, remembered, that Conrad really had been drunk, that he couldn't really have been responsible for anything he'd said or done that night. He probably wouldn't remember it tomorrow. It would be like it had never happened.

As soon as we got inside, I ran up to my room. I wanted to forget what had happened in the car and only remember the way Cam had looked at me, on the stairs with his arm touching my shoulder.

chapter *twenty-four*

The next day, nothing. It wasn't that he ignored me, because that would have been something. Some kind of proof that it had happened, that something had changed. But no, he treated me the same. Like I was still little Belly, the girl with the messy flyaway ponytail and the bony knees, running after them on the beach. I should have known better.

The thing was, whether he was pushing me away or pulling me toward him, I was still going in the same direction. Toward Conrad.

Cam didn't call me for a few days. Not that I blamed him. I didn't call him either—although I thought about it. I just didn't know what to say.

When he finally called, he didn't bring up the party. He asked me to go to the drive-in. I said yes. Right away

I worried, though—did going to the drive-in mean we were going to have to make out? Like, crazy make out, steamed windows and seats all the way back?

Because that was what people did at the drive-in. There were the families, and then there were the hot and heavy couples toward the back of the lot. I'd never been part of a couple before. I'd gone as a family, with Susannah and my mother and everyone, and I'd gone with the boys, but never as a couple, like on a date.

Once, Jeremiah and Steven and I went and spied on Conrad on one of his dates. Susannah let Jeremiah drive us, even though he only had a permit. The drive-in was three miles away, and at Cousins, everyone drove, even kids on their parents' laps. Conrad had been furious when he'd caught us spying on him. He'd been on his way to the concession stand when he saw us. It had been pretty funny—his hair was all messed up as he yelled at us, and his lips were rosy and they had a glossy sheen. Jeremiah cracked up the whole time.

I wished Steven and Jeremiah were out there in the dark somewhere, spying on us and cracking up. It would make me feel comforted somehow. Safer.

I was wearing Cam's hoodie, and I kept it zipped all the way to my neck. I sat with my arms crossed, like I was shivering. Even though I liked Cam, even though I wanted to be there, I had the sudden urge to jump out of the car and walk home. I'd only ever kissed one boy, and that hadn't been for real. Taylor called me the nun. Maybe I was one, at heart. Maybe I should have joined a convent. I didn't even know if this was an actual date. Maybe he'd been so turned off by me the other night that all he wanted was to be my friend.

Cam tuned the radio until he found the right station. Drumming his hands on the steering wheel, he said, "Do you want any popcorn or anything?"

I kind of did, but I didn't want it to get stuck in my teeth, so I said no, thanks.

He was pretty into the movie, the way he leaned up close to the windshield to get a closer look sometimes. It was an old horror movie, one that Cam told me was really famous, but I'd never heard of it. I was barely paying attention anyway—I felt like I was watching him way more than I was watching the movie. He licked his lips a lot. He didn't look over and laugh with me during the funny parts the way Jeremiah did. He just sat on his side of the car, leaned up against the door, as far away from me as possible.

When the movie was over, he started the car up. "Ready?" he said.

I felt a wave of disappointment. He was taking me home already. He wasn't going to take me to Scoops for an ice cream cone, or a hot fudge sundae to share. The date, if you could even call it that, had been a failure. He didn't try to make out with me once. Not that I knew if I'd even have let him, but still. He could've at least tried.

"Um-hmm," I said. I felt like I might cry, and I wasn't quite sure why, when I hadn't even been sure if I wanted to kiss him in the first place.

We drove home in silence. He parked the car in front of the house—I held my breath a little, my hand on the door handle, waiting to see if he'd turn off the ignition or if I should hop out. But he turned it off and leaned his head back against the headrest a second.

"Do you know why I remembered you?" he asked me suddenly.

It was a question so out of nowhere that it took me a little while to figure out what he was talking about.

"You mean from Latin Convention?"

"Yeah."

"Was it my Coliseum model?" I was only half-joking. Steven had helped me build it; it had been pretty impressive.

"No." Cam ran his hand through his hair. He wouldn't look at me. "It's because I thought you were really pretty. Like, maybe the prettiest girl I'd ever seen."

I laughed. In the car, it sounded really loud. "Yeah, right. Nice try, Sextus."

"I mean it," he insisted, his voice rising.

"You're making that up." I didn't believe it could be true. I didn't want to let myself believe it. With the boys any compliment like this would always be the first part of a joke.

He shook his head, lips tight. He was offended that I didn't believe him. I hadn't meant to hurt his feelings. I just didn't see how it could be true. It was almost mean of him to lie about it. I knew what I looked like back then, and I wasn't the prettiest girl *anybody* had ever seen, not with my thick glasses and chubby cheeks and little-girl body.

Cam looked me in the eyes then. "The first day, you wore a blue dress. It was, like, corduroy or something. It made your eyes look really blue."

"My eyes are gray," I said.

"Yes, but that dress made them look blue."

Which was why I wore it. It was my favorite. I wondered where it was now. Probably packed up in the attic back home, with all my winter clothes. It was too small now anyway.

He looked so sweet, the way he watched me, waiting for my reaction. His cheeks were flushed peach. I swallowed hard and said, "Why didn't you come up to me?"

He shrugged. "You were always with your friends. I watched you that whole week, trying to get up the nerve. I couldn't believe it when I saw you at the bonfire that night. Pretty bizarre, huh?" Cam laughed, but he sounded embarrassed.

"Pretty bizarre," I echoed. I couldn't believe he'd noticed me. With Taylor by my side, who would have even bothered to look at me?

"I almost messed up my Catullus speech on purpose, so you'd win," he said, remembering. He inched a little closer to me.

"I'm glad you didn't," I said. I reached out and touched his arm. My hand shook. "I wish you had come up to me."

That's when he dipped his head low and kissed me. I didn't let go of the door handle. All I could think was, *I wish this had been my first kiss.*

chapter *twenty-five*

When I went into the house, I was walking on cotton candy and clouds, replaying everything that had just happened—until I heard my mother and Susannah arguing in the living room. Fear seized up inside of me; it felt like a fist clenched tight around my heart. They never fought, not really. I'd only ever seen them fight one time. It was last summer. The three of us had gone shopping to this fancy mall an hour away from Cousins. It was an outdoor mall, the kind where people bring their pocket-size dogs on fancy leashes. I saw this dress—it was a purpley plum chiffon, with little off the shoulder straps, way too old for me. I loved it. Susannah said I should try it on, just for fun, so I did. She took one look at me and said I had to have it. My mother shook her head right away. She said, "She's fourteen. Where will she wear a dress like that?" Susannah said it didn't matter, that it was made for me. I knew we couldn't afford it, my mother was newly divorced, after all, but I still pleaded with her. I begged. They got into an argument right there in the boutique, in front of people. Susannah wanted to buy it for me, and my mother wouldn't let her. I told them never mind, I didn't want it, even though I did. I knew my mother was right, I'd never wear it.

When we got back from Cousins at the end of summer, I found the dress in my suitcase, wrapped in paper and packed neatly on top like it had always been there. Susannah had gone back and bought it for me. It was so like her to do that. Later, my mother must have seen it hanging up in my closet, but she never said anything.

Standing there in the foyer, listening, I felt like the spy Steven was always accusing me of being. But I couldn't help it.

I heard Susannah say, "Laurel, I'm a big girl now. I need you to stop trying to manage my life. I'm the one who gets to decide how I want to live it."

I didn't wait for my mother's response. I walked right in and said, "What's going on?" I looked at my mother when I said it, and I knew I sounded like I was blaming her, but I didn't care.

"Nothing. Everything's fine," my mother said, but her eyes looked red and tired.

"Then why were you fighting?"

"We weren't fighting, hon," Susannah assured me. She reached out and smoothed my shoulder, like she was ironing out wrinkled silk. "Everything really is fine."

"It didn't sound like it."

"Well, it is," Susannah told me.

"Promise?" I asked. I wanted to believe her.

"Promise," she said without hesitation.

My mother walked away from us, and I could see from the stiffness of her shoulders that everything was not fine, that she was still upset. But because I wanted to stay with Susannah, where everything really was fine, I didn't follow her. My mother was the kind of person who would rather be alone anyway. Just ask my father.

"What's the matter with her?" I whispered to Susannah.

"It's nothing. Tell me about your date with Cam," she said, leading me to the wicker couch in the sunroom.

I should have kept pressing her, should have tried to figure out what had really happened between the two of them, but my worry was already fading away. I wanted to tell her everything about Cam, everything. Susannah had that way about her, where you wanted to tell her all your secrets and everything in between.

She sat on the couch and patted her lap. I sat down next to her and put my head in her lap and she smoothed my hair away from my forehead. Everything felt safe and cozy, like that fight hadn't happened. And maybe it hadn't even been a fight, maybe I'd misread the whole thing. "Well, he's different from anyone I've ever met," I began.

"How so?"

"He's just so smart, and he doesn't care what people think. And he's so good-looking. I can't even believe he pays me any attention."

Susannah shook her head. "Oh, please. Of course he should pay you attention. You're so lovely, darling. You've really blossomed this summer. People can't *help* but pay you attention."

"Ha," I said, but I felt flattered. She was so good at making people feel special. "I'm glad I have you to talk to about this kind of stuff."

"I am too. But you know, you could talk to your mother."

"She wouldn't be interested in any of it, not really. She'd pretend to care, but she wouldn't."

"Oh, Belly. That's not true. She would care. She does care." Susannah cradled my face in her hands. "Your mother is your biggest fan, next to me. She cares about everything you do. Don't shut her out."

I didn't want to talk about my mother anymore. I wanted to talk about Cam. "You'll never believe what Cam said to me tonight," I began.

chapter *twenty-six*

Just like that, July turned into August. I guessed summer went by a lot faster when you had someone to spend it with. For me, that someone was Cam. Cam Cameron.

Mr. Fisher always came the first week of August. He'd bring Susannah's favorites from the city, almond croissants and lavender chocolates. And flowers, he always brought flowers. Susannah loved flowers. She said she needed them like air, to breathe. She had more vases than I could count, tall ones and fat ones and glass ones. They were all over the house, flowers in vases in every room. Her favorites were peonies. She kept them on her nightstand in her bedroom, so they were the first thing she saw in the morning.

Shells, too. She loved shells. She kept them in hurricane glasses. When she'd come back from a walk on the beach, she'd always come back with a handful of shells. She'd arrange them on the kitchen table, admire them first, say things like, "Doesn't this one look just like an ear?" Or, "Isn't this one the perfect shade of pink?" Then she'd put them in order from biggest to smallest. It was one of her rituals, something I loved to watch her do.

That week, right around when Mr. Fisher usually came, Susannah mentioned that he couldn't get away from work. There had been some sort of emergency at the bank. It would just be the five of us finishing out the summer. It would be the first year without Mr. Fisher and my brother.

After she went to bed, early, Conrad said to me, conversationally, "They're getting a divorce."

"Who?" I said.

"My parents. It's about time."

Jeremiah glared at him. "Shut up, Conrad."

Conrad shrugged. "Why? You know it's true. Belly's not surprised, are you, Belly?"

I was. I was really surprised. I said, to both of them, "I thought they seemed like they were really in love."

Whatever love was, I was sure they had it. I thought they had it a million times over. The way they gazed at each other at the dinner table, how excited Susannah got when he came to the summer house. I didn't think people like that got divorced. People like my parents got divorced. Not Susannah and Mr. Fisher.

"They *were* in love," Jeremiah told me. "I don't really know what happened."

"Dad's a dick. That's what happened," Conrad said, getting up. He sounded so blasé and matter-of-fact, but that didn't seem right. Not when I knew he adored his dad. I wondered if Mr. Fisher had a new girlfriend the way my father did. I wondered if he'd cheated on Susannah. But who would ever cheat on Susannah? It was impossible.

"Don't tell your mom you know," Jeremiah said suddenly. "Mom doesn't know we know."

"I won't," I said. I wondered how they'd found out. My parents had sat Steven and me down and told us everything, explained it all in detail.

As Conrad left, Jeremiah said to me, "Before we left, our dad had been sleeping in the guest room for weeks. He's already moved out most of his clothes. They think we're retarded or something, for us not to notice." His voice cracked at the last part.

I grabbed his hand and squeezed it. He was really hurting. I guessed maybe Conrad was too, even if he didn't show it. It all made sense, when I thought about it. The way Conrad had been acting, so different, so lost. So un-Conrad-like. He was suffering. And then there was Susannah. The way she'd been spending so much time in bed, the way she seemed so sad. She was hurting too.

chapter *twenty-seven*

"You and Cam have been spending a lot of time together," my mother said, looking at me over her newspaper.

"Not really," I said, even though we had been. At the summer house one day just kind of melted into the next; you didn't notice time passing. Cam and I had been hanging out for two weeks before I realized it: He was kind of my boyfriend. We'd spent practically every day together. I didn't know what I'd done before I'd met him. My life must have been really boring.

My mother said, "We miss you around the house." If Susannah had said it, I'd have been flattered, but from my mother it was just really annoying. It felt like recrimination. And anyway, it wasn't like they'd been around so much either. They were always off doing things, just the two of them.

"Belly, will you bring this boy of yours to dinner tomorrow night?" Susannah asked me sweetly.

I wanted to say no, but for me, saying no to Susannah was impossible. Especially with her going through a divorce. I couldn't say no. So instead I said, "Um . . . maybe . . ."

"Please, honey? I'd really like to meet him."

I caved. "All right, I'll ask. I can't promise he doesn't have plans, though."

Susannah nodded serenely. "As long as you ask."

Unfortunately for me, Cam didn't have plans.

Susannah cooked; she made a tofu stir-fry because Cam was a vegetarian. Again, it was something I'd admired about him, but when I saw the look Jeremiah gave me, it made me shrink a little. Jeremiah cooked hamburgers that night—he liked any excuse to use the grill, just like his dad. He asked me if I wanted one too, and I said no even though I did.

Conrad had already eaten and was upstairs playing his guitar. He couldn't even be bothered to eat with us. He came down to get a bottled water, and he didn't even say hello to Cam.

"So why don't you eat meat, Cam?" Jeremiah asked, stuffing half his burger into his mouth.

Cam swallowed his water and said, "I'm morally opposed to eating animals."

Jeremiah nodded seriously. "But Belly eats meat. You let her kiss you with those lips?" Then he cracked up. Susannah and my mother exchanged a knowing kind of smile.

I could feel my face getting hot, and I could feel how tense Cam was beside me. "Shut up, Jeremiah."

Cam glanced at my mother and laughed uneasily. "I don't judge people who choose to eat meat. It's a personal choice."

Jeremiah continued, "So you don't mind when her lips touch dead animal and then they touch your, um, lips?"

Susannah chuckled lightly and said, "Jere, give the guy a break."

"Yeah, Jere, give the guy a break," I said, glaring at him. I kicked him under the table, hard. Hard enough to make him flinch.

"No, it's fine," Cam said. "I don't mind at all. In fact—" Then he pulled me to him and kissed me quickly, right in front of everyone. It was only a peck, but it was embarrassing.

"Please don't kiss Belly at the dinner table," said Jeremiah, gagging a little for effect. "You're making me nauseous."

My mother shook her head at him and said, "Belly's allowed to kiss." Then she pointed her fork at Cam. "But that's it."

She burst out laughing like it was the funniest thing

she'd ever said, and Susannah tried not to smile and told her to hush. I wanted to kill my mother and then myself. "Mom, please. You're so not funny," I said. "No more wine for Mom." I refused to look anywhere near Jeremiah's direction, or Cam's, for that matter.

The truth was, Cam and I hadn't done much else besides kiss. He didn't seem to be in any big hurry. He was careful with me, sweet—nervous even. It was completely different from the way I'd seen other guys behave with girls. Last summer I caught Jeremiah with a girl on the beach, right outside of the house. They were frantic, like if they hadn't been wearing clothes, they'd already have been having sex. I gave him hell for it the whole rest of the summer, but he didn't really care. I wished Cam would care a little more.

"Belly, I'm kidding. You know I'm open to you exploring yourself," my mother said, taking a long sip of chardonnay.

Jeremiah busted out laughing. I stood up and said, "That's it. Cam and I are eating our dinner on the porch." I grabbed my plate and waited for Cam to stand up too.

But he didn't. "Belly, calm down. Everybody's just joking around," he said, loading up his fork with rice and bok choy and shoveling it into his mouth.

"Way to keep her in check, Cam," Jeremiah said, nodding at him. He really did look kind of impressed.

I sat back down, although it killed me to do it. I hated

losing face in front of everyone, but if I did walk out by myself, I knew no one would come after me. I would just be little Belly Button, off pouting again. That was my name when I was being a baby, Belly Button—Steven thought he was such a genius for thinking that one up. "No one keeps me in check, Jeremiah. Least of all Cam Cameron."

Everyone hooted and hollered then, even Cam, and all of a sudden, it was all very normal, like he really belonged there. I could feel myself start to relax. It was all going to be okay. Great, in fact. Amazing, just like Susannah had promised.

After dinner, Cam and I took a walk on the beach. For me there was—is—nothing better than walking on the beach late at night. It feels like you could walk forever, like the whole night is yours and so is the ocean. When you walk on the beach at night, you can say things you can't say in real life. In the dark you can feel really close to a person. You can say whatever you want.

"I'm really glad you came," I told him.

He took my hand and said, "Me too. I'm glad you're glad."

"Of course I'm glad."

I let go of his hand to roll up the bottoms of my jeans, and he said, quietly, "It didn't seem like you were that glad."

"Well, I am." I looked up at him and gave him a quick kiss. "See? This is me, being glad."

He smiled and we started walking again. "Good. So which one of those guys was your first kiss?"

"I told you that?"

"Yup. You said your first kiss was a boy at the beach when you were thirteen."

"Oh." I looked up at his face in the moonlight, and he was still smiling. "Guess."

Immediately he said, "The older one, Conrad."

"Why'd you guess him?"

He shrugged. "Just a feeling, the way he looks at you."

"He hardly looks at me at all," I told him. "And you're wrong, Sextus. It was Jeremiah."

chapter *twenty-eight*

AGE 14

"Truth or dare?" Taylor asked Conrad.

"I'm not playing," he said.

Taylor pouted. "Don't be so gay," she said.

Jeremiah said, "You shouldn't use the word 'gay' like that."

Taylor opened her mouth and closed it. Then she said, "I didn't mean anything by it, Jeremy. I just meant he's being lame."

"Well, 'gay' doesn't mean 'lame,' Taylor, now does it?" Jeremiah said. He spoke in a sarcastic tone, but even mean attention was better than no attention. Probably he was just mad about all the attention she'd been giving Conrad that day.

Taylor heaved a great big sigh and turned to Conrad.

"Conrad, you're being very lame. Play truth or dare with us."

He ignored her and turned the volume on the TV up louder. Then he pretended to mute her with the remote, which made me laugh out loud.

"Fine, he's out. Steven, truth or dare."

Steven rolled his eyes. "Truth."

Taylor's eyes lit up. "Okay. How far did you go with Claire Cho?" I knew she'd been saving that one up for a long time, waiting for the exact moment she could ask. Claire Cho was a girl that Steven had dated for most of freshman year. Taylor swore Claire had cankles, but I thought Claire's ankles were perfectly slim. I thought Claire Cho was kind of perfect.

Steven actually blushed. "I'm not answering that."

"You have to. It's truth or dare. You can't sit here and listen to other people tell secrets if you're not going to," I said. I had been wondering about him and Claire too.

"Nobody's even told any secrets yet!" he protested.

"We're about to, Steven," Taylor said. "Now man up and tell us."

"Yeah, Steven, man up," Jeremiah chimed in.

We all started to chant, "Man up! Man up!" Even Conrad turned the TV on mute to hear the answer.

"Fine," Steven said. "If you shut up, I'll tell you."

We shut right up and waited. "Well?" I said.

"Third," he said at last.

I relaxed back into the couch. Third base. Wow. Interesting. My brother had been to third base. Weird. Gross.

Taylor looked pink with satisfaction. "Well done, Stevie."

He shook his head at her and said, "Now it's my turn." He looked around the room, and I sank deep into the couch cushions. I really, really hoped he wasn't going to pick me and make me say it out loud—how I hadn't even so much as kissed a boy yet. Knowing Steven, he would.

He surprised me when he said, "Taylor. Truth or dare?" He was actually playing along.

Automatically she said, "You can't pick me because I just asked you. You have to pick someone else." Which was true, that was the rule.

"Are you scared, Tay-Tay? Why don't you man up?"

Taylor hesitated. "Fine. Truth."

Steven grinned evilly. "Who would you kiss in this room?"

Taylor considered it for a few seconds, and then she got that cat-that-ate-the-canary look on her face. It was the same look she'd had on her face when she'd dyed her little sister's hair blue when we were eight. She waited until she had everyone's attention, and then she said, triumphantly, "Belly."

There was a stunned kind of silence for a minute, and then everyone started to laugh, Conrad loudest. I threw a pillow at Taylor, hard.

"That's not fair. You didn't answer for real," Jeremiah said, shaking his finger at her.

"Yes, I did," Taylor said smugly. "I pick Belly. Take a closer look at everybody's favorite little sister, Jeremy. She's turning hot before your very eyes."

I hid my face behind a pillow. I knew I was blushing even harder than Steven had. Mostly because it wasn't true, I wasn't turning hot before anyone's eyes, and we all knew it. "Taylor, shut up. Please shut up."

"Yes, please shut up, Tay-Tay," Steven said. He looked kind of red too.

"If you're so serious, then kiss her," said Conrad, his eyes still on the TV.

"Hey," I said, glaring at him. "I'm a person. You can't just kiss me without my permission."

He looked at me and said, "I'm not the one who wants to kiss you."

Hotly, I said, "Either way, permission not granted. To either of you." I wished I could stick my tongue out at him without being accused of being a big baby.

Taylor broke in quickly. She said, "I picked truth, not dare. That's why we're not kissing right now."

"We're not kissing right now because I don't want to kiss you," I told her. I felt flushed, partly because I was mad, and partly because I was flattered. "Now let's stop talking about it. It's your turn to ask."

"Fine. Jeremiah. Truth or dare."

"Dare," he said, leaning against the couch lazily.

"Okay. Kiss somebody in this room, right now." Taylor looked at him confidently and waited.

It felt like the whole room was sitting on the edge of its seat while we waited for Jeremiah to say something. Would he actually do it? He was not the kind of guy to pass up a dare. I, for one, was curious about what kind of kisser he'd be, if he'd go for a French or if he'd give her a quick peck. I also wondered if it would be their first kiss, or if they'd kissed sometime earlier in the week, like at the arcade when I wasn't looking, maybe. I was pretty sure they had.

Jeremiah sat up straight. "Easy," he said, rubbing his hands together with a smile. Taylor smiled back and tilted her head to the side so her hair fell in her eyes just a little bit.

Then he leaned over to me and said, "Ready?" and before I could answer, he kissed me right on the lips. His mouth was a little bit open, but it wasn't a French kiss or anything. I tried to push him off, but he kept on kissing me, for a few more seconds.

I pushed him off again, and he leaned back into the couch, as casual as can be. Everyone else was sitting there with their mouths hanging open, except for Conrad, who didn't even look surprised. But then, he never looked surprised. I, on the other hand, was finding it kind of hard to breathe. I had just had my first kiss. In front of people. In front of my brother.

I couldn't believe that Jeremiah had stolen my first kiss like that. I had been waiting, wanting it to be special, and it had happened during a game of truth or dare. How unspecial could you get? And to top it all off, he had only done it to make Taylor jealous, not because he liked me.

It had worked. Her eyes were narrowed, and she was staring at Jeremiah like he had thrown down some kind of gauntlet. Which, I guess he kind of had.

"Gross," Steven said. "This game is gross. I'm outta here." Then he looked at all of us disgustedly and left.

I got up too, and so did Conrad. "See ya," I said. "And, Jeremiah, I'm getting you back for that."

He winked and said, "A back rub should make us about even," and I threw a pillow directly at his head and slammed the door behind me. The fact that he was being fake-flirty was the worst part. It was so patronizing, so demeaning.

It took me about three seconds before I realized that Taylor wasn't coming after me. She was inside, laughing at Jeremiah's dumb jokes.

In the hallway, Conrad gave me his trademark knowing look and said, "You know you loved it."

I glared at him. "How would you know? You're too obsessed with yourself to notice anybody else."

He walked away from me and said over his shoulder, "Oh, I notice everything, Belly. Even poor little you."

"Screw you!" I said, because that was all I could think

of. I could hear him chuckling as he shut his bedroom door.

I went back to my room and got under the covers. I closed my eyes and replayed and replayed what had just happened. Jeremiah's lips had touched my lips. My lips were no longer my own. They had been touched. By *Jeremiah*. I had finally been kissed, and it was my friend Jeremiah who'd been the one to do it. My friend Jeremiah who had been ignoring me that whole week.

I wished I could talk to Taylor. I wished we could talk about my first kiss, but we couldn't, because right this minute she was downstairs kissing the same boy who had just kissed me. I was sure of it.

When she came back upstairs an hour later, I pretended I was sleeping.

"Belly?" she whispered across the room.

I didn't say anything, but I stirred a little, for effect.

"I know you're still awake, Belly," she said. "And I forgive you."

I wanted to sit right up and say, "You forgive me? Well, I don't forgive you, for coming here and ruining my whole summer." But I didn't say any of it. I just kept fake-sleeping.

The next morning I woke up early, just after seven, and Taylor was already gone. I knew where she was. She'd gone to watch the sunrise with Jeremiah. We'd been planning to go watch the sunrise on the beach one morning before she left, but we always overslept. It was her second to last morning, and she'd chosen Jeremiah. Figured.

I changed into my bathing suit and headed for the pool. In the mornings it was always a little cold outside, just a little bit of bite to the air, but I didn't mind. Swimming in the mornings made me feel like I was swimming in the ocean even when I wasn't. In theory swimming in the ocean sounds great and all, but the salt water burned my eyes too much to do it every day. Plus, the pool was more private, more my own. Even though everyone else swam in it too, in the mornings and at night I had it pretty much to myself, besides Susannah.

When I opened the gate to the pool, I saw my mother sitting in one of the lounge chairs reading a book. Except she wasn't really reading it. She was more just holding it and staring off into space.

"Hi, Mom," I said, more to break her out of her spell than anything else.

She looked up, startled. "Good morning," she said, clearing her throat. "Did you sleep well?"

I shrugged and dropped my towel onto the chair next to hers. "I guess," I said.

My mother shaded her eyes with her hand and looked up at me. "Are you and Taylor having fun?"

"Tons," I said. "Buckets full."

"Where is Taylor?"

"Who knows?" I said. "Who cares?"

"Are you two fighting?" my mother asked casually.

"No. I'm just starting to wish I hadn't brung her, is all."

"Best friends are important. They're the closest thing to a sister you'll ever have," she told me. "Don't squander it."

Irritably I said, "I haven't squandered anything. Why do you always have to put the blame on me for everything?"

"I'm not blaming you. Why must you always make things about you, dear?" My mother smiled at me in her infuriatingly calm way.

I rolled my eyes and jumped backward into the pool. It was freezing cold. When I came up to the surface, I yelled, "I don't!"

Then I started my laps, and whenever I thought about Taylor and Jeremiah, I got madder and pushed harder. By the time I was done, my shoulders burned.

My mother had left, but Taylor and Jeremiah and Steven were just coming in.

"Belly, if you swim too much, you'll get those broad swimmer's shoulders," Taylor warned, dipping her foot in the water.

I ignored her. What did Taylor know about exercise? She thought walking around the mall in high heels was exercise. "Where were you guys?" I asked, floating on my back.

"Just hanging out," Jeremiah said vaguely.

Judas, I thought. A bunch of Benedict Arnolds. "Where's Conrad?"

"Who knows? He's too cool to hang out," Jeremiah said, falling onto a lounge chair.

"He went running," Steven said, a tad defensively. "He has to get in shape for football season. He has to leave for practice next week, remember?"

I remembered. That year Conrad had to leave early so he could get back in time for tryouts. He'd never seemed like the football type to me, but there he was, trying out for the team. I guessed Mr. Fisher had a lot to do with it; he was exactly the type. So was Jeremiah. Although he'd never take it seriously. He never took anything seriously.

"I'll probably play for the team next year too," Jeremiah said casually. He sneaked a peek at Taylor to see if she looked impressed. She didn't. She wasn't even looking at him.

His shoulders sagged a little, and I felt sorry for him despite myself.

I said, "Jere, race me, okay?"

He shrugged and stood up, taking off his shirt. Then he walked over to the deep end and dove in. "You want a handicap?" he asked when he emerged up top.

"No. I think I can beat you without one," I said, paddling over.

"Whoo-hoo! Let's see."

We raced across the length of the pool, freestyle, and he beat me the first time, and then the second. But I wore him down by the third and fourth and beat him too. Taylor cheered me on, which only annoyed me more.

The next morning she was gone again. This time, though, I was gonna join them. It wasn't like she and Jeremiah owned the beach. I had just as much right as they did to watch the sunrise. I got up, put my clothes on, and headed outside.

I didn't see them at first. They were farther down than usual, and they had their backs to me. He had his arms around her, and they were kissing. They weren't even watching the sunrise. And . . . it wasn't Jeremiah, either. It was Steven. My brother.

It was just like in those movies with the surprise ending, where everything falls into place and clicks. Suddenly my life had become *The Usual Suspects*, and Taylor, Taylor was Keyser Soze. The scenes ran through the mind—Taylor and Steven bickering, the way he had come to the boardwalk that night, Taylor claiming that Claire Cho had cankles, all the afternoons she'd spent at my house.

They didn't hear me walk up. But then I said, loudly, "Wow, so first Conrad, then Jeremiah, and now my brother."

She turned around, surprised, and Steven looked surprised too. "Belly—," she started.

"Shut up." I looked at my brother then, and he squirmed. "You're a hypocrite. You don't even like her! You said she bleached out all her brain cells with her Sun-In!"

He cleared his throat. "I never said that," he said, glancing back and forth between Taylor and me. Her eyes had welled up, and she was wiping her left eye with the back of her sweatshirt sleeve. *Steven's* sweatshirt sleeve. I was too angry to cry.

"I'm telling Jeremiah."

"Belly, just freakin' calm down. You're too old for your temper tantrums," Steven said, shaking his head in his brotherly way.

The words came out of me, hot and fast and sure. "Go to hell." I had never talked like that to my brother before. I don't think I'd ever talked like that to *anyone* before. Steven blinked.

That's when I started to walk away, and Taylor chased after me. She had to run to catch up, that's how fast I was walking. I guess anger gives you speed.

"Belly, I'm so sorry," she began. "I was going to tell you. Things just happened really fast."

I stopped walking and spun around. "When? When did they happen? Because from what I saw, things were happening so fast with *Jeremy*, not with my older brother."

She shrugged helplessly, which only made me madder. Poor helpless little Taylor. "I've always had a crush on Steven. You know that, Belly."

"Actually, I didn't. Thanks for telling me."

"When he liked me back, it was like, I couldn't believe it. I didn't think."

"That's the thing. He doesn't like you. He's just using you because you're around," I said. I knew it was cruel, but I also knew it was true. Then I walked into the house and left her standing outside.

She chased after me and grabbed my arm, but I shrugged her off.

"Please don't be mad, Belly. I want things to stay the same with us forever," Taylor said, brown eyes brimming with tears. What she really meant was, I want you to stay the same forever while I grow bigger breasts and quit violin and kiss your brother.

"Things can't stay the same forever," I said. I was saying it to hurt her because I knew it would.

"Don't be mad at me, okay, Belly?" she pleaded. Taylor hated it when people were mad at her.

"I'm not mad at you," I said. "I just don't think we really know each other anymore."

"Don't say that, Belly."

"I'm only saying it because it's true."

She said, "I'm sorry, okay?"

I looked away for a second. "You promised you'd be nice to him."

"Who? Steven?" Taylor looked genuinely confused.

"No. Jeremiah. You said you'd be nice."

She waved her hand in the air. "Oh, he doesn't care."

"Yeah, he does. It's just that you don't know him." Like I do, I wanted to add. "I didn't think you'd ever act so—so . . ." I searched for the perfect word, to cut her the way she'd cut me. "Slutty."

"I'm not a slut," she said in a tiny voice.

So this was my power over her, my supposed innocence over her supposed sluttiness. It was all such BS. I would've traded my spot for hers in a second.

Later, Jeremiah asked me if I wanted to play spit. We hadn't played once all summer. It used to be our thing, our tradition. I was grateful to have it back. Even if it was a consolation prize.

He dealt me my hand, and we began to play, but both of us were just going through the motions. We had other things on our minds. I thought that we had this unspoken agreement not to talk about her, that maybe he didn't even know what had happened, but then he said, "I wish you never brought her."

"Me too."

"It's better when it's just us," he said, shuffling his stack.

"Yeah," I agreed.

After she left, after that summer, things were the same and they weren't. She and I were still friends, but not best friends, not like we used to be. But we were still friends.

She'd known me my whole life. It's hard to throw away history. It was like you were throwing away a part of yourself.

Steven went right back to ignoring Taylor and obsessing over Claire Cho. We just pretended like none of it had ever happened. But it did.

chapter *twenty-nine*

I heard him come home. I think the whole house must have—except for Jeremiah, who could sleep through a tidal wave. Conrad made his way up the stairs, tripping and cursing, and then he shut his door and turned on his stereo, loud. It was three in the morning.

I lay in bed for about three seconds before I leapt up and ran down the hallway to his room. I knocked, twice, but the music was so loud I doubted he could hear anything. I opened the door. He was sitting on the edge of his bed, taking his shoes off. He looked up and saw me standing there. "Didn't your mom teach you to knock?" he asked, getting up and turning down the stereo.

"I did, but your music was so loud you couldn't hear me. You probably woke up the whole house, Conrad." I stepped inside and closed the door behind me. I hadn't been in his room in a long time. It was the same as I remembered, perfectly neat. Jeremiah's looked like hurricane season, but not Conrad's. In Conrad's room there was a place for everything, and everything was in its place. His pencil drawings, still tacked onto the bulletin board, his model cars still lined up on the dresser. It was comforting to see that at least that was still the same.

His hair was messed up, like someone had been running their hands through it. Probably Red Sox girl. "Are you going to tell on me, Belly? Are you still a tattletale?"

I ignored him and walked over to his desk. Hanging right above it there was a framed picture of him in his football uniform, the football tucked under his arm. "Why'd you quit, anyway?"

"It wasn't fun anymore."

"I thought you loved it."

"No, it was my dad who loved it," he said.

"It seemed like you did too." In the picture he looked tough, but I could tell he was trying not to smile.

"Why'd you quit dance?"

I turned around and looked at him. He was unbuttoning his work shirt, a white button-down, and he had on a T-shirt underneath.

"You remember that?"

"You used to dance all around the house like a little gnome."

I narrowed my eyes at him. "Gnomes don't dance. I was a ballerina, for your information."

He smirked. "So why'd you quit, then?"

It had been around the time my parents got divorced. My mom couldn't pick me up and drop me off twice a week all on her own. She had a job. It just didn't seem worth it anymore. I was bored of it by then anyway, and Taylor wasn't doing it anymore either. Also, I hated the way I looked in my leotard. I got boobs before the whole rest of the class, and in our class picture I looked like I could be the teacher. It was embarrassing.

I didn't answer his question. Instead I said, "I was really good! I could have been dancing in a company by now!" I couldn't have. I wasn't that good, not by any stretch of the imagination.

"Right," he said mockingly. He looked so smug sitting there on the bed.

"At least I can dance."

"Hey, I can dance," he protested.

I crossed my arms. "Prove it."

"I don't have to prove it. I taught you some moves, remember? How quickly we forget." Conrad jumped up off the bed and grabbed my hand and twirled me around. "See? We're dancing."

His arm was slung around my waist, and he laughed before he let me go. "I'm a better dancer than you, Belly," he said, collapsing onto his bed.

I stared at him. I didn't get him at all. One minute he was broody and withdrawn, and the next he was laughing and twirling me around the room. "I don't consider that dancing," I said. I backed out of the room. "And can you keep your music down? You already woke up the whole house."

He smiled. Conrad had a way of looking at me, at you, at anybody, that made everything unravel and want to fall at his feet. He said, "Sure. Good night, Bells." Bells, my nickname from a thousand years ago.

He made it so hard not to love him. When he was sweet like this, I remembered why I did. Used to love him, I mean.

I remembered everything.

chapter *thirty*
AGE 11

The summer house had a stack of CDs that we listened to, and that was pretty much it. We spent the whole summer listening to the same CDs. There was the Police, which Susannah put on in the morning; there was Bob Dylan, which she put on in the afternoon; and there was Billie Holiday, which she put on at dinner. The nights were a free-for-all. It was the funniest thing. Jeremiah would put on his Chronic CD, and my mother would be doing laundry, humming along. Even though she hated gangster rap. And then my mother might put on her Aretha Franklin CD, and Jeremiah would sing all the words, because we all knew them by that time, we'd heard it so much.

My favorite music was the Motown and the beach

music. I would listen to it on Susannah's old Walkman when I tanned. That night I put the *Boogie Beach Shag* CD on the big stereo in the living room, and Susannah grabbed Jeremiah and started to dance. He'd been playing poker with Steven and Conrad and my mother, who was very, very good at poker.

At first Jeremiah protested, but then he was dancing too. It was called the shag, and it was a 1960s kind of beach dance. I watched them, Susannah throwing her head back and laughing, and Jeremiah twirling her around, and I wanted to dance too. My feet positively itched to dance. I did dance ballet and modern, after all. I could show off how good I was.

"Stevie, dance with me," I demanded, poking him with my big toe. I was lying down on the floor, on my stomach, looking up at them.

"Yeah, right," he said. Not that he even knew how.

"Connie, dance with Belly," Susannah urged, her face flushed as Jeremiah twirled her again.

I didn't dare look at Conrad. I was afraid my love for him and my need for him to say yes would be written on my face like a poem.

Conrad sighed. He was still big on doing the right thing then. So he gave me his hand and pulled me up. I got to my feet shakily. He didn't let go of my hand. "This is how you shag," he said, shuffling his feet from side to side. "One-two-three, one-two-three, rock step."

It took me a few tries to get it. It was harder than it looked, and I was nervous. "Get on the beat," Steven said from the sidelines.

"Don't look so uptight, Belly. It's a relaxed kind of dance," my mother said from the couch.

I tried to ignore them and look only at Conrad. "How did you learn this?" I asked him.

"My mom taught both of us," Conrad said simply. Then he brought me in close and positioned my arms around his so we stepped together, side by side. "This is called the cuddle."

The cuddle was my favorite part. It was the closest I had ever been to him. "Let's do it again," I said, pretending to be confused.

He showed me again, putting his arm over mine. "See? You're getting it now."

He spun me around, and I felt dizzy. With pure, absolute joy.

chapter *thirty-one*

I spent the whole next day in the ocean with Cam. We packed a picnic. Cam made avocado and sprout sandwiches with Susannah's homemade mayonnaise and whole wheat bread. They were good, too. We stayed in the ocean for what felt like hours at a time. Every time a wave began to crest, one of us would start to laugh, and then we'd get overtaken by the wave and water. My eyes burned from the salty seawater, and my skin felt raw from scraping against the sand so many times, like I'd scrubbed my whole body with my mother's St. Ives Apricot Scrub. It was pretty great.

After, we stumbled back to our towels. I loved getting cold and wet in the ocean and then running back to the towels and letting the sun bake the sand off. I could do it all day—ocean, sand, ocean, sand.

I'd packed strawberry Fruit Roll-Ups, and we ate them so quick my teeth hurt. "I love Fruit Roll-Ups," I said, reaching for the last one.

He snatched it away. "So do I, and you already had three and I only had two," he said, peeling away the plastic sheet. He grinned and dangled it above my mouth.

"You have three seconds to hand it over," I warned. "I don't care if you had two Fruit Roll-Ups and I had twenty. It's my house."

Cam laughed and popped the whole thing into his mouth. Chewing loudly, he said, "It's not your house. It's Susannah's house."

"Shows how much you know. It's *all* of our house," I said, falling back on my towel. I was suddenly really thirsty. Fruit Roll-Ups will do that. Especially when you have three in about three minutes. Squinting up at him, I said, "Will you go back to *our* house and get some Kool-Aid? Pretty please?"

"I don't know anyone who consumes more sugar than you do in one day," Cam said, shaking his head at me sadly. "White sugar is evil."

"Says the guy who just ate the last Fruit Roll-Up," I countered.

"Waste not, want not," he said. He stood up and brushed the sand off his shorts. "I'll bring you water, not Kool-Aid."

I stuck my tongue out at him and rolled over. "Just be quick about it," I said.

He wasn't. He was gone forty-five minutes before I headed back to the house, loaded up with our towels and sunscreen and trash, breathing hard and sweating like a camel in the desert. He was in the living room, playing video games with the boys. They were all lying around in their swimming trunks. We pretty much stayed suited up all summer.

"Thanks for never coming back with my Kool-Aid," I said, tossing my beach bag onto the ground.

Cam looked up from his game guiltily. "Whoops! My bad. The guys asked me to play, so . . ." He trailed off.

"Don't apologize," Conrad advised him.

"Yeah, what are you, her slave? Now she's got you making her Kool-Aid?" Jeremiah said, jamming his thumb into the controller. He turned around and grinned at me to show me he was kidding, but I didn't grin back to show him it was okay.

Conrad didn't say anything, and I didn't even look at him. I could feel him looking at me, though. I wished he'd stop.

Why was it that even when I had my own friend I still felt left out of their club? It wasn't fair. It wasn't fair that Cam was so grateful to be a part of it all. The day had been so good, too.

"Where's my mom and Susannah?" I snapped.

"They went off somewhere," Jeremiah said vaguely. "Shopping, maybe?"

My mother hated shopping. Susannah must have dragged her.

I stalked off to the kitchen for my Kool-Aid. Conrad got up and followed me. I didn't have to turn around to know it was him.

I went about my business, pouring myself a tall glass of grape Kool-Aid and pretending he wasn't standing there watching me. "Are you just going to ignore me?" he finally said.

"No," I said. "What do you want?"

He sighed and came closer. "Why do you have to be like that?" Then he leaned forward, close, too close. "Can I have some?"

I put the glass on the counter and started to walk away, but he grabbed my wrist. I think I might have gasped. He said, "Come on, Bells."

His fingers felt cool, the way he always was. Suddenly I felt hot and feverish. I snatched my hand away. "Leave me alone."

"Why are you mad at me?" He had the nerve to look genuinely confused and also anxious. Because for him, the two things were connected—if he was confused, he was anxious. And he was hardly ever confused, so then he was hardly ever anxious. He'd certainly never been anxious over me. I was inconsequential to him. Always had been.

"Do you honestly care?" I could feel my heart thudding hard in my chest. I felt prickly and strange, waiting for his answer.

"Yes." Conrad looked surprised, like he couldn't believe he cared either.

The problem was, I didn't entirely know. I guessed it was mostly the way he was making me feel all mixed-up inside. Being nice to me one minute and cold the next. He made me remember things I didn't want to remember. Not now. Things were really going well with Cam, but every time I thought I was sure about him, Conrad would look at me a certain way, or twirl me, or call me Bells, and it all went to crap.

"Oh, why don't you go smoke a cigarette," I said.

The muscle in his jaw twitched. "Okay," he said.

I felt a mixture of guilt and satisfaction that I had finally gotten to him. And then he said, "Why don't you go look at yourself in the mirror some more?"

It was like he had slapped me. It was mortifying, being caught out and having someone see the bad things about you. Had he caught me looking at myself in the mirror, checking myself out, admiring myself? Did everyone think I was vain and shallow now?

I closed my lips tight and backed away from him, shaking my head slowly.

"Belly—," he started. He was sorry. It was written all over his face.

I walked into the living room and left him standing there. Cam and Jeremiah stared at me like they knew something was up. Had they heard us? Did it even matter?

"I get next game," I said. I wondered if this was the way old crushes died, with a whimper, slowly, and then, just like that—gone.

chapter *thirty-two*

Cam came over again, and he stayed till late. Around midnight I asked him if he wanted to go for a walk on the beach. So we did, and we held hands, too. The ocean looked silver and bottomless, like it was a million years old. Which I guessed it was.

"Truth or dare?" he asked me.

I wasn't in the mood for real truths. An idea came to me, from out of nowhere. The idea was this: I wanted to go skinny-dipping. With Cam. That was what older kids did at the beach, just like hooking up at the drive-in. If we went skinny-dipping, it would be like proof. That I had grown up.

So I said, "Cam, let's play Would You Rather. Would you rather go skinny-dipping right this second, or . . ." I was having trouble thinking of an "or."

"The first one, the first one," he said, grinning. "Or both, whatever the second one is."

Suddenly I felt giddy, almost drunk. I ran away from him, toward the water, and threw my sweatshirt into the sand. I had on my bikini underneath my clothes. "Here are the rules," I called out, unbuttoning my shorts. "No nakedness until we're fully submerged! And no peeking!"

"Wait," he said, running up to me, sand flying everywhere. "Are we really doing this?"

"Well, yeah. Don't you want to?"

"Yeah, but what if your mom sees us?" Cam glanced back toward the house.

"She won't. You can't see anything from the house; it's too dark."

He glanced at me and then back at the house again. "Maybe later," he said doubtfully.

I stared at him. Wasn't he the one who was supposed to be convincing me? "Are you serious?" What I really wanted to say was, Are you gay?

"Yeah. It's not late enough. What if people are still awake?" He picked up my sweatshirt and handed it to me. "Maybe we can come back later."

I knew he didn't mean it.

Part of me was mad, and part of me was relieved. It was like craving a fried peanut butter and banana sandwich and then realizing two bites in that you didn't want it after all.

I snatched my sweatshirt from him and said, "Don't do me any favors, Cam." Then I walked away as fast as I could, and sand kicked up behind me. I thought he might follow me, but he didn't. I didn't look back to see what he was doing either. He was probably sitting in the sand writing one of his stupid poems by the light of the moon.

As soon as I got back inside, I stormed into the kitchen. There was one light on; Conrad was sitting at the table spooning into a watermelon. "Where's Cam Cameron?" he asked wryly.

I had to think for a second about whether he was being nice or making fun of me. His expression looked normal and bland, so I took it as a little of both. If he was going to pretend our fight from before hadn't happened, then so would I.

"Who knows," I said, rummaging around the fridge and pulling out a yogurt. "Who cares?"

"Lover's spat?"

The smug look on his face made me want to slap him. "Mind your own business," I said, sitting down next to him with a spoon and a container of strawberry yogurt. It was Susannah's fat-free stuff, and the top looked watery and solid. I closed the foil flap on the yogurt and pushed it away.

Conrad pushed the watermelon over to me. "You shouldn't be so hard on people, Belly." Then he stood up and said, "And put your shirt on."

I scooped out a chunk of watermelon and stuck my tongue out at his retreating figure. Why did he make me feel like I was still thirteen? In my head I heard my mother's voice—"Nobody can make you feel like anything, Belly. Not without your permission. Eleanor Roosevelt said that. I almost named you after her." Blah, blah, blah. But she was kind of right. I wasn't giving him permission to make me feel bad, not anymore. I just wished my hair had at least been wet, or I'd had sand in my clothes, so he could have thought we'd been up to something, even if we hadn't been.

I sat at the table and ate watermelon. I ate it until I had scooped out half of the middle. I was waiting for Cam to come back inside, and when he didn't, I only felt madder. Part of me was tempted to lock the door on him. He'd probably meet some random homeless guy and become best friends with him, and then he'd tell me the man's life story the next day. Not that there were any homeless guys on our end of the beach. Not that I'd ever seen a homeless person in Cousins, for that matter. But if there was, Cam would find him.

Only, Cam didn't come back to the house. He just left. I heard his car start, watched from the downstairs hallway as he backed down the driveway. I wanted to run after his car and yell at him. He was supposed to come back. What if I'd ruined things and he didn't like me anymore? What if I never saw him again?

That night I lay in bed, thinking about how summer romances really do happen so fast, and then they're over so fast.

But the next morning, when I went to the deck to eat my toast, I found an empty water bottle on the steps that led down to the beach. Poland Spring, the kind Cam was always drinking. There was a piece of paper inside, a note. A message in a bottle. The ink was a little smeared, but I could still read what it said. It said, "IOU one skinny-dip."

chapter *thirty-three*

Jeremiah told me I could come hang by the pool while he lifeguarded. I'd never been inside the country club pool. It was huge and fancy, so I jumped at the chance. The country club seemed like a mysterious place. Conrad hadn't let us come the summer before; he'd said it would be embarrassing.

Midafternoon, I rode my bike over. Everything there was lush and green; it was surrounded by a golf course. There was a girl at a table with a clipboard, and I went over and told her I was there to see Jeremiah, and she waved me in.

I spotted Jeremiah before he saw me. He was sitting in the lifeguard chair, talking to a dark-haired girl in a white bikini. He was laughing, and so was she. He looked so important in the chair. I'd never seen him at an actual job before.

Suddenly I felt shy. I walked over slowly, my flip-flops slapping along the pavement. "Hey," I said when I was a few feet away.

Jeremiah looked down from his chair and grinned at me. "You came," he said, squinting at me and shielding his eyes with his hands like a visor.

"Yup." I swung my canvas bag back and forth, like a pendulum. The bag had my name on it in cursive. It was from L.L.Bean, a gift from Susannah.

"Belly, this is Yolie. She's my co-lifeguard."

Yolie reached over and shook my hand. It struck me as a businessy thing to do for someone in a bikini. She had a firm handshake, a nice grip, something my mother would have appreciated. "Hi, Belly," she said. "I've heard a lot about you."

"You have?" I looked up at Jeremiah.

He smirked. "Yeah. I told her all about the way you snore so loud that I can hear you down the hall."

I smacked his foot. "Shut up." Turning to Yolie, I said, "It's nice to meet you."

She smiled at me. She had dimples in both cheeks and a crooked bottom tooth. "You too. Jere, do you want to take your break now?"

"In a little bit," he said. "Belly, go work on your sun damage."

I stuck my tongue out at him and spread out my towel on a lounge chair not too far away. The pool was a perfect turquoise, and there were two diving boards, one high and one low. There were a ton of kids splashing around inside, and I figured I'd swim too when I got too hot to stand it. I just lay there with my sunglasses on and my eyes closed, tanning and listening to my music.

Jeremiah came over after a while. He sat on the edge of my chair and drank from my thermos of Kool-Aid. "She's pretty," I said.

"Who? Yolie?" He shrugged. "She's nice. One of my many admirers."

"Ha!"

"So what about you? Cam Cameron, huh? Cam the vegetarian. Cam the straight edge."

I tried not to smile. "So what? I like him."

"He's kind of a dork."

"That's what I like about him. He's . . . different."

He frowned slightly. "Different from who?"

"I don't know." But I did know. I knew exactly who he was different from.

"You mean he's not a dick like Conrad?"

I laughed, and so did he. "Yeah, exactly. He's nice."

"Just nice, huh?"

"More than nice."

"So you're over him, then? For real?" We both knew the "him" he was talking about.

"Yes," I told him.

"I don't believe you," Jeremiah said, watching me

closely—just like when he was trying to figure out what kind of hand I had in Uno.

I took off my sunglasses and looked him in the eye. "It's true. I'm over him."

"We'll see," Jeremiah said, standing up. "My break's over. Are you okay over here? Wait around and I'll drive us home. I can put your bike in the back."

I nodded, and watched him walk back to the lifeguard chair. Jeremiah was a good friend. He'd always been good to me, watched out for me.

chapter *thirty-four*

My mother and Susannah sat in beach chairs, and I lay on an old Ralph Lauren teddy bear towel. It was my favorite one because it was extra long, and soft from so many washings.

"What are you up to tonight, bean?" my mother asked me. I loved it when she called me bean. It reminded me of being six years old and falling asleep in her bed.

Proudly I told them, "Me and Cam are going to Putt Putt."

We used to go all the time as kids. Mr. Fisher would take us, and he was always pitting the boys against one another. "Twenty dollars for the first one to get a hole in one." "Twenty dollars for the winner." Steven loved it. I think he wished Mr. Fisher was our dad. He actually could've been. Susannah told me my mother had dated him first, but my mother had handed him over to Susannah because she knew they'd be perfect together.

Mr. Fisher included me in the mini golf competitions, but he never expected me to win. Of course I never did. I hated mini golf anyway. I hated the little pencils and the fake turf. It was all so annoyingly perfect. Kind of like Mr. Fisher. Conrad wanted so badly to be like him, and I used to hope he never would. Be like him, I mean.

The last time I had been to Putt Putt was when I was thirteen and I'd gotten my period for the first time. I was wearing white cutoffs, and Steven had been scared. He'd thought I had cut myself or something—for a second, I'd thought so too. After that, after getting my period by the fourth hole, I never wanted to go back. Not even when the boys invited me. So going with Cam felt like I was reclaiming Putt Putt, taking it back for my twelve-year-old self. It had even been my idea to go.

My mother said, "Can you be home early? I want us to spend a little time together, maybe watch a movie."

"How early? You guys go to bed at, like, nine."

My mother took her sunglasses off and looked at me. She had two indentations on her nose where her glasses had been. "I wish you'd spend more time at the house."

"I'm at the house right now," I reminded her.

She acted like she didn't hear me. "You've been spending so much time with this person—"

"You said you liked him!" I looked at Susannah for

support, and she looked back at me sympathetically.

My mother sighed, and Susannah broke in then, saying, "We do like Cam. We just miss you, Belly. We completely accept the fact that you have an actual life." She adjusted her floppy straw hat and winked at me. "We just want you to include us a little bit!"

I smiled in spite of myself. "Okay," I said, lying back down on the towel. "I'll come home early. We'll watch a movie."

"Done," my mother said.

I closed my eyes and put my headphones on. Maybe she had a point. I had been spending all my time with Cam. Maybe she really did miss me. It was just, she couldn't take for granted that I was going to spend every night at home like I had every other summer. I was almost sixteen, practically an adult. My mother had to accept that I couldn't be her bean forever.

They thought I was asleep when they started talking. But I wasn't. I could hear what they were saying, even over the music.

"Conrad's been behaving like a little shit," my mother said in a low voice. "He left all these beer bottles out on the deck this morning for me to clean up. It's getting out of hand."

Susannah sighed. "I think he knows something's up. He's been like this for months now. He's so sensitive, I know it's going to hit him harder."

"Don't you think it's time you told the boys?" Whenever my mother said "Don't you think," all she really meant was, "I think. So you should too."

"When the summer's over. That's soon enough."

"Beck," my mother began, "I think it might be time."

"I'll know when it's time," Susannah said. "Don't push me, Laur."

I knew there was nothing my mother could say that would change her mind. Susannah was soft, but she was resolute, stubborn as a mule when she wanted to be. She was pure steel underneath all her softness.

I wanted to tell them both, Conrad knows already and so does Jeremiah, but I couldn't. It wouldn't be right. It wasn't my business to tell.

Susannah wanted it to be some kind of perfect summer, where the parents were still together and everything was the way it had always been. Those kinds of summers don't exist anymore, I wanted to tell her.

chapter *thirty-five*

Around sunset, Cam came and picked me up for mini golf. I waited for him on the front porch, and when he pulled into the driveway, I ran up to his car. Instead of going to the passenger side, I walked right around to the driver's side. "Can I drive?" I asked. I knew he'd say yes.

He shook his head at me and said, dryly, "How does anybody ever say no to you?"

I batted my eyelashes at him. "No one ever does," I said, even though it wasn't true, not even a little bit.

I opened the car door, and he scooted over.

Backing out of the driveway, I told him, "I have to be home early tonight."

"No problem." He cleared his throat. "And, um, can you slow down a little? The speed limit is thirty-five on this road."

As I drove, he kept looking over at me and smiling. "What? Why are you smiling?" I asked. I felt like covering my face up with my T-shirt.

"Instead of a ski-slope nose, you have, like, a little bunny slope." He reached over and tapped it. I slapped his hand away.

"I hate my nose," I told him.

Cam looked perplexed. "Why? Your nose is cute. It's the imperfections that make things beautiful."

I wondered if that meant he thought I was beautiful. I wondered if that was why he liked me, my imperfections.

We ended up staying out later than I'd planned. The people in front of us took forever on each hole; they were a couple, and they kept stopping to kiss. It was annoying. I wanted to tell them, Mini golf is not where you go to hook up. That's what the drive-in's for. And then after, Cam was hungry, so we stopped for fried clams, and by that time it was after ten, and I knew my mother and Susannah would already be asleep.

He let me drive home. I didn't even have to ask; he just handed me the keys. In the driveway when we got home, I turned off the ignition. All of the lights in the house were off except for Conrad's. "I don't want to go inside yet," I told Cam.

"I thought you had to be home early."

"I did. I do. I'm just not ready to go inside yet." I turned on the radio, and we sat there for five minutes listening.

Then Cam cleared his throat and said, "Can I kiss you?"

I wished he hadn't asked. I wished he'd just done it. Asking made everything feel awkward; it put me in a position where I had to say yes. I wanted to roll my eyes at him but instead I said, "Um, okay. But next time, please don't ask. Asking someone if they want to kiss you is weird. You're supposed to just do it."

I regretted saying it right away, as soon as I saw the look on Cam's face. "Never mind," he said, red-faced. "Forget I asked."

"Cam, I'm sorr—" Before I could finish, he leaned over and kissed me. His cheek was stubbly and it felt kind of rough but nice.

When it was over, he said, "Okay?"

I smiled and said, "Okay." I unbuckled my seat belt. "Good night."

Then I got out of the car, and he came around and took the driver's seat. We hugged, and I found myself wishing that Conrad was watching. Even though it didn't matter, even though I didn't even like him anymore. I just wanted him to know I didn't like him anymore, to really know it. To see it with his own two eyes.

I ran up to the front door, and I didn't have to turn around to know that Cam would wait until I was inside before he drove away.

The next day my mother didn't mention anything, but she didn't have to. She could make me feel guilty without saying a word.

chapter *thirty-six*

My birthday always marked the beginning of the end of summer. It was my final thing to look forward to. And this summer I was turning sixteen. Sweet sixteen was supposed to be special, a really big deal—Taylor was renting out a reception hall for hers, and her cousin was DJ-ing and she was inviting the whole school. She'd had it planned for ages. My birthdays here were always the same: cake; gag gifts from the boys; and looking through all the old photo albums, with me sandwiched between Susannah and my mom on the couch. Every birthday I've ever had has been here, in this house. There are pictures of my mother sitting on the porch pregnant, with a glass of iced tea and a wide brimmed hat, and there's me, inside her belly. There are pictures of the four of us, Conrad, Steven, Jeremiah, and me, running around on the beach—I was naked except for my birthday hat, chasing after them. My mother didn't put me in a bathing suit until I was four years old. She just let me run around wild.

I didn't expect this birthday to be any different. Which, was comforting and also kind of depressing. Except, Steven wouldn't be there—my first birthday without him trying to elbow in and blow out my candles before I could.

I already knew what my parents were giving me: Steven's old car; they were getting it detailed with a new paint job and everything. When I got back to school, I would take driver's ed, and soon I wouldn't have to ask for a ride ever again.

I couldn't help but wonder if anyone back home remembered it was my birthday. Besides Taylor. She remembered; she always did. She called me at exactly 9:02 in the morning to sing happy birthday, every year. That was nice and all, but the trouble with having a summer birthday and being away was you couldn't have a party with all your school friends. You didn't get the balloons taped to your locker or any of it. I'd never really minded, but just then I did, a little.

My mother told me I could invite Cam over. But I didn't. I didn't even tell him it was my birthday. I didn't want him to feel like he had to do something. But it was more than that. I figured that if this birthday was going to be like every other one, I might as well really have it be like every other one. It should just be us, my summer family.

When I woke up that morning, the house smelled like butter and sugar. Susannah had baked a birthday cake. It was three layers and it was pink with a white border. She wrote in loopy white frosting HAPPY BIRTH-DAY, BELLS. She'd lit a few sparkler candles on top, and they sizzled and sparked like mad fireflies. She and my mother started to sing, and Susannah gestured for Conrad and Jeremiah to join in. They both did, off-key and obnoxious.

"Make a wish, Belly," my mother said.

I was still in my pajamas, and I couldn't stop smiling. The past four birthdays I had wished for the same thing. Not this year. This year I would wish for something else. I watched the sparklers die down, and then I closed my eyes and blew.

"Open my present first," Susannah urged. She thrust a small box wrapped in pink paper into my hands.

My mother looked at her questioningly. "What did you do, Beck?"

She smiled a mysterious smile and squeezed my wrist. "Open it, honey."

I ripped the paper off and opened the box. It was a pearl necklace, a whole strand of tiny creamy white pearls with a shiny gold clasp. It looked old, not like something you could buy today. It was like my father's Swiss grand-father clock, beautifully crafted, right down to the clasp. It was the prettiest thing I'd ever seen.

"Oh my gosh," I breathed, lifting it up.

I looked at Susannah, who was beaming, and then at my mother, who I thought would say it was much too extravagant, but she didn't. She smiled and said, "Are those—"

"Yes." Susannah turned to me and said, "My father gave me those for my sixteenth birthday. I want you to have them."

"Really?" I looked back at my mother, to make sure it was okay. She nodded. "Wow, thank you, Susannah. They're beautiful."

She took them from me and fastened them around my neck. I'd never worn pearls before. I couldn't stop touching them.

Susannah clapped her hands. She didn't like to linger too much after she'd given a gift; she just enjoyed the giving of it. "Okay, what's next? Jeremiah? Con?"

Conrad shifted uncomfortably. "I forgot. Sorry, Belly."

I blinked. He'd never forgotten my birthday before. "That's okay," I said. I couldn't even look at him.

"Open mine next," Jeremiah said. "Although, after that, mine kind of sucks in comparison. Thanks a lot, Mom." He handed me a small box and leaned back in his chair.

I shook the box. "Okay, what could it be? Plastic poop? A license plate key chain?"

He smiled. "You'll see. Yolie helped me pick it out."

"Who's Yolie?" Susannah asked.

"A girl who's in love with Jeremiah," I said, opening the box.

Inside, nestled on a bed of cotton, was a small charm, a tiny silver key.

chapter *thirty-seven*
AGE 11

"Happy birthday, butthead," Steven sang, dumping a pail full of sand into my lap. A sand crab wriggled out of the sand and crawled onto my thigh. I let out a shriek and jumped up. I chased Steven down the beach, white hot fury pumping through my veins. I wasn't fast enough to catch him; I never was. He ran circles around me.

"Come and blow out your candles," my mother called.

As soon as Steven turned around to head back to the towel, I leapt onto his back and with one arm around his neck, I pulled his hair as hard as I could.

"Ow!" he howled, stumbling. I clung to his back like a monkey, even with Jeremiah grabbing my foot and trying to pull me off. Conrad fell to his knees, laughing.

"Children," Susannah called. "There's cake!"

I hopped off of Steven's back and scrambled over to the blanket.

"I'm gonna get you!" he yelled, chasing after me.

I hid behind my mother. "You can't. It's my birthday." I stuck my tongue out at him. The boys fell onto the blanket, wet and sandy.

"Mom," Steven complained. "She pulled out a hunk of my hair."

"Steven, you have a whole head full. I wouldn't worry about it." My mother lit the candles on the cake she'd baked that morning. It was a lopsided Duncan Hines yellow cake with chocolate frosting. She had messy handwriting, so "Happy Birthday" looked like "Happy Bimday."

I blew out the candles before Steven could try to "help" me. I didn't want him stealing my wish. I wished for Conrad, of course.

"Open your presents, Smelly," Steven said sullenly. I already knew what he'd gotten me. A stick of deodorant. He'd wrapped it in Kleenex; I could see right through the tissue.

I ignored him and reached for a small flat box wrapped in seashell paper. It was from Susannah, so I knew it would be good. I tore off the wrapping paper, and inside there was a silver charm bracelet, from the store Susannah loved, Rheingold's, where they sold fancy china and crystal candy dishes. On the bracelet there were five charms: a conch shell, a bathing suit, a sand castle, a pair of sunglasses, and a horseshoe.

"For how lucky we are to have you in our lives," Susannah said, touching the horseshoe.

I lifted it up, and the charms glinted and sparkled in the sunlight. "I love it."

My mother was silent. I knew what she was thinking. She was thinking that Susannah had overdone it, that she'd spent too much money. I felt guilty for loving the bracelet so much. My mother had bought me sheet music and CDs. We didn't have as much money as they did, and in that moment I finally understood what that meant.

chapter *thirty-eight*

"I love it," I said.

I ran upstairs to my room and went straight for the music box on my dresser, where I kept my charm bracelet. I grabbed the bracelet and ran back downstairs.

"See?" I said, putting the key charm on and fastening it onto my wrist.

"It's a key, because you'll be driving soon. Get it?" Jeremiah said, leaning back in his chair and clasping his hands behind his head.

I got it. I smiled to show him I did.

Conrad leaned in for a closer look. "Nice," he said.

I held it in the palm of my other hand. I couldn't stop looking at it. "I love it," I said again. "But it's from Rheingold's. It must have been really expensive."

"I saved up all summer to buy it," he said solemnly.

I stared at him. "No, you didn't!"

He broke into a smile. "Fooled ya. Gullible as ever, aren't you?"

Punching him on the arm, I said, "I didn't believe you anyway, jerk." Even though I had, for a second.

Jeremiah rubbed his arm where I'd punched it. "It wasn't that expensive. Anyway, I'm big-time now, remember? Don't worry about me. I'm just glad you like it. Yolie said you would."

I hugged him fiercely. "It's perfect."

"What a wonderful gift, Jere," Susannah said. "It's better than my old necklace, that's for sure."

He laughed. "Yeah, right," he said, but I could tell he was pleased.

My mother got up and started cutting the cake. She wasn't a very good cake cutter: The pieces were too big, and they fell apart on the sides. "Who wants cake?" she said, licking her finger.

"I'm not hungry," Conrad said abruptly. He stood up, looking at his watch. "I've gotta get dressed for work. Happy birthday, Belly."

He went upstairs, and nobody said anything for a minute. Then my mother said, loudly, "This cake is delicious. Have some, Beck." She pushed a piece in front of her.

Smiling faintly, Susannah said, "I'm not hungry either.

You know what they say about the cook not having a taste for her own cooking. But you guys eat."

I took a big bite. "Mmm. Yellow cake, my favorite."

"From scratch," my mother said.

chapter *thirty-nine*

Conrad invited Nicole, Red Sox girl, over to the house. Our house. I couldn't believe Red Sox girl was at our house. It was bizarre to have a girl there other than me.

It was midafternoon. I was out on the deck, sitting at the patio table, eating a Doritos sandwich when they drove up. She was wearing short shorts and a white T-shirt, and a pair of sunglasses on top of her head. The Red Sox hat was nowhere in sight. She looked chic. She looked like she belonged. Unlike me, in my old Cuz Beach shirt that doubled as a pajama dress. I thought he'd at least bring her inside the house, but they hung out on the other side of the deck, lying on the lounge chairs. I couldn't hear what they were saying, but I could hear her giggling like crazy.

After about five minutes I couldn't take it anymore. I got on the phone and called Cam. He said he'd be over in half an hour, but it was more like fifteen minutes.

They walked back into the house when Cam and I were arguing over which movie to watch. "What are you guys gonna watch?" Conrad asked, sitting on the couch opposite us. Red Sox girl sat next to him. She was practically in his lap.

I didn't look at him when I said, "We're trying to decide." Emphasis on the "we're."

"Can we watch too?" Conrad asked. "You guys know Nicole, right?"

So, suddenly Conrad felt like being social when he'd spent the whole summer locked up in his room?

"Hey," she said in a bored tone.

"Hey," I said, matching her tone as best I could.

"Hey, Nicole," Cam said. I wanted to tell him not to be so friendly, but I knew he wouldn't have listened anyway. "I want to watch *Reservoir Dogs*, but Belly wants to watch *Titanic*."

"Seriously?" the girl said, and Conrad laughed.

"Belly loves *Titanic*," he said mockingly.

"I loved it when I was, like, nine," I said. "I want to watch right now so I can laugh at it, for your information."

I was as cool as a cucumber. I wasn't going to let him

goad me in front of Cam again. And actually, I still loved *Titanic*. What wasn't to love about a doomed romance on a doomed ship? I knew for a fact that Conrad had liked it too, even though he'd pretended not to.

"I vote for *Reservoir Dogs*," Nicole said, examining her fingernails.

Did she even get a vote? What was she doing there anyway?

"Two votes for *Reservoir Dogs*," Cam said. "What about you, Conrad?"

"I think I'll vote for *Titanic*," he said blandly. "*Reservoir Dogs* sucks even harder than *Titanic*. It's overrated."

I narrowed my eyes at him. "You know what? I think I'll change my vote to *Reservoir Dogs*. So it looks like you're outnumbered, Conrad," I said.

Nicole looked up from her fingernails and said, "Well, then, I change my vote to *Titanic*."

"Who are you?" I muttered under my breath. "Does she even get voting privileges here?"

"Does he?" Conrad jerked his elbow at Cam, who looked startled. "Just kidding, man."

"Let's just watch *Titanic*," Cam said, taking the DVD out of its case.

We sat and watched stiffly. Everyone else busted up laughing at the part when Jack stands at the helm and says, "I'm the king of the world." I was silent. About midway through, Nicole whispered something into Conrad's ear, and the two of them stood up. "See you guys later," Conrad said.

As soon as they were gone, I hissed, "They're so disgusting. They probably went upstairs to go at it."

"Go at it? Who says 'go at it'?" Cam said, bemused.

"Shut up. Don't you think she was gross?"

"Gross? No. I think she's cute. A little too much bronzer, maybe."

I laughed in spite of myself. "Bronzer? What do you know about bronzer?"

"I have an older sister, remember," he said, smiling self-consciously. "She likes makeup. We share a bathroom."

I didn't remember Cam saying he had a sister.

"Well, anyway, she does wear too much bronzer. She's bright orange! I wonder where her Red Sox hat is," I mused.

Cam picked up the remote control and paused the movie. "Why are you so obsessed with her?"

"I'm not obsessed with her. Why would I be obsessed with her? She has no personality. She's like one of those pod people. She looks at Conrad like he's God." I knew he was judging me for being so mean, but I couldn't stop talking.

He looked at me like he wanted to say something, but he didn't. Instead he turned the movie back on.

We sat there on the couch and finished watching the movie in silence. Toward the end I heard Conrad's voice on the stairs, and without even thinking I snuggled closer to Cam. I rested my head on his shoulder.

Conrad and Nicole came back downstairs, and Conrad looked at the two of us for a second before saying, "Tell my mom I took Nicole home."

I barely looked up. "Okay."

As soon as they were gone, Cam sat straight up, and I did too. He took a breath. "Did you invite me over here to make him jealous?"

"Who?" I said.

"You know who. Conrad."

I could feel a flush rising up my chest and all the way to my cheeks. "No." It seemed like everybody was wanting to know where things stood with Conrad and me.

"Do you still like him?"

"No."

He let out a breath of air. "See, you hesitated."

"No, I didn't!"

Did I? Had I? I was sure I hadn't. To Cam I said, "When I look at Conrad, all I feel is disgust."

I could tell he didn't believe it. I didn't either. Because the truth was, when I looked at Conrad, all I felt was a yearning that never went away. It was the same as it had always been. Here I had this really great guy who actually liked me, and deep down inside I was still hung up on Conrad. There, that was the real truth. I had never really let go. I was just like Rose on that stupid makeshift raft.

Cam cleared his throat and said, "You're leaving soon. Do you want to keep in touch?"

I hadn't thought about that. He was right, the summer was almost over. Pretty soon I would be home again. "Um . . . do you?"

"Well, yeah. I do."

He looked at me like he was expecting something, and I couldn't figure out what it was for a few seconds. Then I said, "Me too. I do too." But it came too late. Cam took his cell phone out of his pocket and said he'd better get going. I didn't argue.

chapter *forty*

We finally had our movie night. My mother, Susannah, Jeremiah, and I watched Susannah's favorite Alfred Hitchcock movies in the rec room with all the lights off. My mother made kettle corn in the big cast-iron pot, and she went out and bought Milk Duds and gummy bears and saltwater taffy. Susannah loved saltwater taffy. It was classic, like old times, only without Steven and Conrad, who was working a dinner shift.

Halfway through *Notorious*, her most favorite of all, Susannah fell asleep. My mother covered her with a blanket, and when the movie was over, she whispered, "Jeremiah, will you carry her upstairs?"

Jeremiah nodded quickly, and Susannah didn't even wake up when he lifted her in his arms and carried her up the rec room stairs. He picked her up like she was weightless, a feather. I'd never seen him do that before. Even though we were almost the same age, in that moment he almost seemed grown-up.

My mother got up too, stretching. "I'm exhausted. Are you going to bed, too, Belly?"

"Not yet. I think I'll clean up down here first," I said.

"Good girl," she said, winking at me, and then she headed upstairs.

I started picking up the taffy wrappers and a few kernels that had fallen onto the carpet.

Jeremiah came back down when I was putting the movie into its case. He sank into the couch cushions. "Let's not go to sleep yet," he said, looking up at me.

"Okay. Do you wanna watch another movie?"

"Nah. Let's just watch TV." He picked up the remote and started flipping through channels randomly. "Where's Cam Cameron been lately?"

Sitting back down, I sighed a little. "I don't know. He hasn't called, and I haven't called him. The summer's almost over. I'll probably never see him again."

He didn't look at me when he said, "Do you want to? See him again?"

"I don't know. . . . I'm not sure. Maybe. Maybe not."

Jeremiah put the TV on mute. He turned and looked at me then. "I don't think he's the guy for you." His eyes looked somber. I'd never seen him look so somber.

Lightly I said, "Yeah, I doubt it too."

"Belly . . . ," he began. He took a deep breath of air and puffed up his cheeks, and then he blew it out so hard the hair on his forehead fluttered. I could feel my heart start to pound—something was going to happen. He was going to say something I didn't want to hear. He was going to go and change everything.

I opened my mouth to speak, to interrupt him before he said something he couldn't take back, and he shook his head. "Just let me get this out."

He took another deep breath. "You've always been my best friend. But now it's more. I see you as more than that." He continued, scooting closer to me. "You're cooler than any other girl I've ever met, and you're there for me. You've always been there for me. I . . . I can count on you. And you can count on me too. You know that."

I nodded. I could hear him talking, see his lips moving, but my mind was working a million miles a minute. This was Jeremiah. My buddy, my best pal. Practically my brother. The hugeness of it all made it hard to breathe. I could barely look at him. Because I didn't. I didn't see him that way. There was only one person. For me that person was Conrad.

"And I know you've always liked Conrad, but you're over him now, right?" His eyes looked so hopeful, it killed me, killed me to not answer him the way he wanted me to.

"I . . . I don't know," I whispered.

He sucked in his breath, the way he did when he was frustrated. "But why? He doesn't see you that way. I do."

I could feel my eyes starting to tear up, which wasn't fair. I couldn't cry. It was just that he was right. Conrad didn't see me that way. I only wished I could see Jeremiah the way he saw me. "I know. I wish I didn't. But I do. I still do."

Jeremiah moved away from me. He wouldn't look at me; his eyes looked everywhere but at mine. "He'll only end up hurting you," he said, and his voice cracked.

"I'm so, so sorry. Please don't be mad at me. I couldn't take it if you were mad at me."

He sighed. "I'm not mad at you. I'm just—why does it always have to be Conrad?"

Then he got up, and left me sitting there.

chapter *forty-one*
AGE 12

Mr. Fisher had taken the boys on one of their overnight deep-sea fishing trips. Jeremiah couldn't go; he'd been sick earlier that day so Susannah made him stay home. The two of us spent the night on the old plaid couch in the basement eating chips and dip and watching movies.

In between *The Terminator* and *Terminator 2*, Jeremiah said bitterly, "He likes Con better than me, you know."

I had gotten up to change the DVDs, and I turned around and said, "Huh?"

"It's true. I don't really care anyway. I think he's a dick," Jeremiah said, picking at a thread on the flannel blanket in his lap.

I thought he was kind of a dick too, but I didn't say so. You're not supposed to join in when someone is bashing his father. I just put the DVD in and sat back down. Taking a corner of the blanket, I said, "He's not so bad."

Jeremiah gave me a look. "He is, and you know it. Con thinks he's God or something. So does your brother."

"It's just that your dad is so different from our dad," I said defensively. "Your dad takes you guys fishing and, like, plays football with you. Our dad doesn't do that kind of stuff. He likes chess."

He shrugged. "I like chess."

I hadn't known that about him. I liked it too. My dad had taught me to play when I was seven. I wasn't bad either. I had never joined chess club, even though I'd kind of wanted to. Chess club was for the nose-pickers. That's what Taylor called them.

"And Conrad likes chess too," Jeremiah said. "He just tries to be what our dad wants. And the thing is, I don't even think he likes football, not like I do. He's just good at it like he is at everything."

There was nothing I could say to that. Conrad *was* good at everything. I grabbed a handful of chips and stuffed them into my mouth so I wouldn't have to say anything.

"One day I'm gonna be better than him," Jeremiah said.

I didn't see that happening. Conrad was too good.

"I know you like Conrad," Jeremiah said suddenly.

I swallowed the chips. They tasted like rabbit feed all of a sudden. "No, I don't," I said. "I don't like Conrad."

"Yes, you do," he said, and his eyes looked so knowing and wise. "Tell the truth. No secrets, remember?" No secrets was something Jeremiah and I had been saying for pretty much forever. It was a tradition, the same way Jeremiah's drinking my sweet cereal milk was tradition— just one of those things we said to each other when it was just the two of us.

"No, I really don't like him," I insisted. "I like him like a friend. I don't look at him like that."

"Yes, you do. You look at him like you love him."

I couldn't take those knowing eyes looking at me for one more second. Hotly I said, "You just think that because you're jealous of anything Conrad does."

"I'm not jealous. I just wish I could be as good as him," he said softly. Then he burped and turned the movie on.

The thing was, Jeremiah was right. I did love him. I knew the exact moment it became real too. Conrad got up early to make a special belated Father's Day breakfast, only Mr. Fisher hadn't been able to come down the night before. He wasn't there the next morning the way he was supposed to be. Conrad cooked anyway, and he was thirteen and a terrible cook, but we all ate it. Watching him serving rubbery eggs and pretending not to be sad, I thought to myself, *I will love this boy forever.*

chapter *forty-two*

He'd gone running on the beach, something he'd started doing recently—I knew because I'd watched him from my window two mornings in a row. He was wearing gym shorts and a T-shirt; sweat had formed in a circle in the middle of his back. He'd left about an hour before, I'd seen him take off, and he was running back to the house now.

I walked out there, to the porch, without a real plan in my mind. All I knew was that the summer was almost over. Soon it would be too late. We would drive away, and I would never have told him. Jeremiah had laid it all out on the line. Now it was my turn. I couldn't go another whole year not having told him. I'd been so afraid of change, of anything tipping our little summer sailboat—but Jeremiah had already done that, and look, we were still alive. We were still Belly and Jeremiah.

I had to, I had to do it, because to not do it would kill me. I couldn't keep yearning for something, for someone who might or might not like me back. I had to know for sure. Now or never.

He didn't hear me coming up behind him. He was bent down loosening the laces of his sneakers.

"Conrad," I said. He didn't hear me, so I said it again, louder. "Conrad."

He looked up, startled. Then he stood up straight. "Hey."

Catching him off guard felt like a good sign. He had a million walls. Maybe if I just started talking, he wouldn't have time to build up a new one.

I sucked in my lips and began to speak. I said the first words I thought of, the ones that had been on my heart since the beginning. I said, "I've loved you since I was ten years old."

He blinked.

"You're the only boy I've ever thought about. My whole life, it's always been you. You taught me how to dance, you came out and got me the time I swam out too far. Do you remember that? You stayed with me and you pushed me back to shore, and the whole time, you kept saying, 'We're almost there,' and I believed it. I believed it because you were the one who was saying it, and I believed everything you ever said. Compared to you, everyone else is saltines, even Cam. And I hate saltines. You know that. You know everything about me, even this, which is that I really love you."

I waited, standing in front of him. I was out of breath. I felt like my heart would explode, it was so full. I pulled my hair into a ponytail with my hand and held it like that, still waiting for him to say something, anything.

It felt like a thousand years before he spoke.

"Well you shouldn't. I'm not the one. Sorry."

And that was all he said. I let out a big breath of air and stared at him. "I don't believe you," I said. "You like me too; I know it." I'd seen the way he'd looked at me when I was with Cam, I'd seen it with my own two eyes.

"Not the way you want me to," he said. He sighed, and in this sad way, like he felt sorry for me, he said, "You're still such a kid, Belly."

"I'm not a kid anymore! You just wish I was, so that way you wouldn't have to deal with any of it. That's why you've been mad at me this whole summer," I said, my voice getting louder. "You do like me. Admit it."

"You're crazy," he said, laughing a little as he walked away from me.

But not this time. I wasn't going to let him off the hook that easily. I was sick and tired of his brooding James

Dean routine. He had feelings for me. I knew it. I was going to make him say it.

I grabbed his shirt sleeve. "Admit it. You were mad when I started hanging out with Cam. You wanted me to still be your little admirer."

"What?" He shook me off. "Get your head out of your ass, Belly. The world doesn't revolve around you."

My cheeks flamed bright red; I could feel the heat beneath my skin. It was like a sunburn times a million. "Yes, exactly, because the world revolves around *you*, right?"

"You have no idea what you're talking about." There was a warning in his voice, but I didn't stop to listen. I was too mad. I was finally saying what I really thought, and there was no turning back now.

I kept getting in his face. I wasn't going to let him walk away from me, not this time. "You just want to keep me on this hook, right? So I'll keep chasing after you and you can feel good about yourself. As soon as I start to get over you, you just reel me back in. You're so screwed up in the head. But I'm telling you, Conrad, this is it."

He snapped, "What are you talking about?"

My hair whipped around my face as I spun around to walk backward, facing him. "This is it. You don't get to have me anymore. Not as your friend or your admirer or anything. I'm through."

His mouth twisted. "What do you want from me?

You have your little boyfriend to play with now, remember?"

I shook my head and backed away from him. "It's not like that," I said. He'd gotten it all wrong. That wasn't what I was trying to do. He'd been the one stringing *me* along, like, my whole life. He knew how I felt, and he let me love him. He *wanted* me to.

He stepped closer to me. "One minute you like me. Then Cam . . ." Conrad paused. "And then Jeremiah. Isn't that right? You want to have your cake and eat it too, but you also want your cookies, and your ice cream . . ."

"Shut up!" I yelled.

"You're the one who's been playing games, Belly." He was trying to sound casual, offhand, but his body was tense, like every muscle was as tight as his stupid guitar strings.

"You've been an ass all summer. All you think about is yourself. So your parents are getting divorced! So what? People's parents get divorced. It's not an excuse to treat people like crap!"

He snapped his head away from me. "Shut your mouth," he said, and his jaw twitched. I had finally done it. I was getting to him.

"Susannah was crying the other day because of you— she could barely get out of bed! Do you even care? Do you even know how selfish you are?"

Conrad stepped up close to me, so close our faces

were nearly touching, like he might either hit me or kiss me. I could hear my heart pounding in my ears. I was so mad I almost wished he'd hit me. I knew he'd never do it, not in a million years. He grabbed my arms and shook me, and then he let go just as suddenly. I could feel tears building up, because for a second there, I thought he might.

Kiss me.

I was crying when Jeremiah walked up. He'd been at work lifeguarding; his hair was still wet. I didn't even hear his car pull up. He took one look at the two of us, and he knew something bad was happening. He almost looked scared. And then he just looked furious. He said, "What the hell is going on? Conrad, what's your problem?"

Conrad glared at him. "Just keep her away from me. I'm not in the mood to deal with any of this."

I flinched. It was like he really had hit me. It was worse than that.

He started to walk away, and Jeremiah grabbed his arm. "You need to start dealing with this, man. You're acting like a jerk. Quit taking your anger out on everybody else. Leave Belly alone."

I shivered. Was this because of me? All summer, Conrad's moodiness, locking himself up in his room— had it really been because of me? Was it more than just his parents divorcing? Had he been that upset over seeing me with someone else?

Conrad tried to shrug him off. "Why don't *you* leave *me* alone? How about we try that instead?"

But Jeremiah wouldn't let go. He said, "We've been leaving you alone. We've left you alone this whole summer, getting drunk and sulking like a little kid. You're supposed to be the older one, right? The big brother? Act like it, dumbass. Freaking man up and handle your business."

"Get out of my face," Conrad growled.

"No." Jeremiah stepped closer, until their faces were inches apart, just like ours had been not fifteen minutes before.

In a dangerous voice Conrad said, "I'm warning you, Jeremiah."

The two of them were like two angry dogs, growling and spitting and circling each other. They'd forgotten I was there. I felt like I was watching something I shouldn't, like I was spying. I wanted to put my hands over my ears. They'd never been like this with each other in all the time I'd known them. They might have argued, but it had never been like this, not once. I knew I should leave, but I couldn't bring myself to do it. I just stood there on the periphery, holding my arms close to my chest.

"You're just like Dad, you know that?" Jeremiah shouted.

That's when I knew it had nothing to do with me. This was bigger than anything I could be a part of.

This was something I knew nothing about.

Conrad pushed Jeremiah away roughly, and Jeremiah pushed him back. Conrad stumbled and nearly fell, and when he rose up, he punched Jeremiah right in the face. I think I screamed. Then they were wrestling around, grabbing at each other, hitting and cursing and breathing heavy. They knocked over Susannah's big glass jar of sun tea, and it cracked open. Tea spilled out all over the porch. There was blood on the sand. I didn't know whose it was.

They kept fighting, fighting over the broken glass, even though Jeremiah was about to lose his flip-flops. A few times I said, "Stop!" but they couldn't hear me. They looked alike. I'd never noticed how alike they looked. But right then they looked like brothers. They kept struggling until suddenly, in the midst of it all, my mother was there. I guessed she'd come through the other screen door. I don't know—she was just there. She broke the two of them apart with this incredible kind of brute strength, the kind only mothers have.

She held them apart with a hand on each of their chests. "You two need to stop," she said, and instead of sounding mad, she sounded so sad. She sounded like she might cry, and my mother never cried.

They were breathing hard, not looking at each other, but they were connected, the three of them. They understood something I didn't. I was just standing there on the periphery, bearing witness to it all. It was like the time I went to church with Taylor, and everyone else knew all the words to the songs, but I didn't. They lifted their arms in the air and swayed and knew every word by heart, and I felt like an intruder.

"You know, don't you?" my mother said, her hands crumpling away from them.

Jeremiah sucked in his breath, and I knew he was holding it in, trying not to cry. His face was already starting to bruise. Conrad, though, his face was indifferent, detached. Like he wasn't there.

Until his face sort of opened up, and suddenly he looked about eight years old. I looked behind me, and there was Susannah standing in the doorway. She was wearing her white cotton housedress, and she looked so frail standing there. "I'm sorry," she said, lifting her hands up helplessly.

She stepped toward the boys, hesitant, and my mother backed away. Susannah held out her arms and Jeremiah fell right in, and even though he was so much bigger than she was, he looked small. Blood from his face smeared over the front of her dress, but they didn't pull away. He cried like I hadn't heard him cry since Conrad had accidentally closed the car door on his hand years and years ago. Conrad had cried just as hard as Jeremiah had that day, but this day he didn't. He let Susannah touch his hair, but he didn't cry.

"Belly, let's go," my mother said, taking my hand. She

hadn't done that in a very long time. Like a little kid, I followed her inside. We went upstairs, to her room. She closed the door and sat down on the bed. I sat down next to her.

"What's happening?" I asked her, faltering, searching her face for some kind of answer.

She took my hands and put them in hers. She held them tight, like she was the one holding on to me and not the other way around. She said, "Belly, Susannah's sick again."

I closed my eyes. I could hear the ocean roaring all around me; it was like holding a conch shell up to my ear really close. It wasn't true. It wasn't true. I was anywhere but there, in that moment. I was swimming under a canopy of stars; I was at school, sitting in math class; on my bike, on the trail behind our house. I wasn't there. This wasn't happening.

"Oh, bean," my mother sighed. "I need you to open your eyes. I need you to hear me."

I wouldn't open them; I wouldn't listen. I wasn't even there.

"She's sick. She has been for a long time. The cancer came back. And it's—it's aggressive. It's spread to her liver."

I opened my eyes and snatched my hands away from her. "Stop talking. She's not sick. She's fine. She's still Susannah." My face was wet and I didn't even know when I had started to cry.

My mother nodded, wet her lips. "You're right. She's still Susannah. She does things her way. She didn't want you kids to know. She wanted this summer to be— perfect." Her voice caught on the word "perfect." Like a run in a stocking, it caught, and she had tears in her eyes too.

She pulled me to her, held me against her chest and rocked me. And I let her.

"But they did know," I whimpered. "Everybody knew but me. I'm the only one who didn't know, and I love Susannah more than anybody."

Which wasn't true, I knew that. Jeremiah and Conrad, they loved her best of all. But it felt true. I wanted to tell my mother that it didn't matter anyway, Susannah had had cancer last time and she'd been fine. She'd be fine again. But if I said it out loud, it would be like admitting that she really did have cancer, that this really was happening. And I couldn't.

That night I lay in bed and cried. My whole body ached. I opened all the windows in my room and lay in the dark, just listening to the ocean. I wished the tide would carry me out and never bring me back. I wondered if that was how Conrad felt, how Jeremiah felt. How my mother felt.

It felt like the world was ending and nothing would ever be the same again. It was, and it wouldn't.

chapter *forty-three*

When we were little and the house was full, full of people like my father and Mr. Fisher and other friends, Jeremiah and I would share a bed and so would Conrad and Steven. My mother would come and tuck us in. The boys would pretend they were too old for it, but I knew they liked it just as much as I did. It was that feeling of being snug as a bug in a rug, cuddly as a burrito. I'd lie in bed and listen to the music drifting up the steps from downstairs, and Jeremiah and I would whisper scary stories to each other till we fell asleep. He always fell asleep first. I'd try to pinch him awake, but it never worked. The last time that happened might have been the last time I ever felt really, really safe in the world. Like all was right and sound.

The night of the boys' fight, I knocked on Jeremiah's door. "Come in," he said.

He was lying in bed staring at the ceiling with his hands clasped behind his head. His cheeks were wet and his eyes looked wet and red. His right eye was purpley gray, and it was already swelling up. As soon as he saw me, he rubbed his eyes with the back of his hand.

"Hey," I said. "Can I come in?"

He sat up. "Yeah, okay."

I walked over to him and sat on the edge of the bed with my back pushed up against the wall. "I'm sorry," I began. I'd been practicing what I would say, how I would say it, so he would know how sorry I was. For everything. But then I started to cry and ruined it.

He reached over and kneaded my shoulder awkwardly. He could not look at me, which in a way was easier. "It's not fair," I said, and then I began to weep.

Jeremiah said, "I've been thinking about it all summer, how this is probably the last one. This is her favorite place, you know. I wanted it to be perfect for her, but Conrad went and ruined everything. He took off. My mom's so worried, and that's the last thing she needs, to be worrying about Conrad. He's the most selfish person I know, besides my dad."

He's hurting too, I thought, but I didn't say it out loud because it wouldn't help anything. So I just said, "I wish I had known. If I had been paying attention, it would have been different."

Jeremiah shook his head. "She didn't want you to know.

She didn't want any of us to know. She wanted it to be like this, so we pretended. For her. But I wish I could have told you. It might have been easier or something." He wiped his eyes with his T-shirt collar, and I could see him trying so hard to keep it together, to be the strong one.

I reached for him, to hug him, and he shuddered, and something seemed to break inside of him. He began to cry, really cry, but quietly. We cried together, our shoulders shaking and shuddering with the weight of all of it. We cried like that for a long time. When we stopped, he let go of me and wiped his nose.

"Scoot over," I said.

He scooted closer to the wall, and I stretched my legs out next to him. "I'm sleeping in here, okay," I said, but it wasn't a question.

Jeremiah nodded and we slept like that, in our clothes on top of the comforter. Even though we were older, it felt just the same. We slept face-to-face, the way we used to.

I woke up early the next morning clinging to the side of the bed. Jeremiah was sprawled out and snoring. I covered him with my side of the comforter, so he was tucked in like with a sleeping bag. Then I left.

I headed back to my room, and I had my hand on the doorknob when I heard Conrad's voice. "Goood morning," he said. I knew right away he'd seen me leave Jeremiah's room.

Slowly I turned around. And there he was. He was standing there in last night's clothes, just like me. He looked rumpled, and he swayed just slightly. He looked like he was going to throw up.

"Are you drunk?"

He shrugged like he couldn't care less, but his shoulders were tense and rigid. Snidely he said, "Aren't you supposed to be nice to me now? Like the way you were for Jere last night?"

I opened my mouth to defend myself, to say that nothing had happened, that all we'd done was cry ourselves to sleep. But I didn't want to. Conrad didn't deserve to know anything. "You're the most selfish person I ever met," I said slowly and deliberately. I let each word puncture the air. I had never wanted to hurt somebody so bad in my whole life. "I can't believe I ever thought I loved you."

His face turned white. He opened and then closed his mouth. And then he did it again. I'd never seen him at a loss for words before.

I walked back to my room. It was the first time I'd ever gotten the last word with Conrad. I had done it. I had finally let him go. It felt like freedom, but freedom bought at some bloody, terrible price. It didn't feel good. Did I even have a right to say those things to him, with him hurting the way he was? Did I have any rights to him at all? He was in pain, and so was I.

When I got back into bed, I got under the covers and

cried some more, and here I was thinking I didn't have any more tears left. Everything was wrong.

How could it be that I had spent this whole summer worrying about boys, swimming, and getting tan, while Susannah was sick? How could that be? The thought of life without Susannah felt impossible. It was inconceivable; I couldn't even picture it. I couldn't imagine what it would be like for Jeremiah and Conrad. She was their mother.

Later that morning I didn't get out of bed. I slept until eleven, and then I just stayed there. I was afraid to go downstairs and face Susannah and have her see that I knew.

Around noon my mother bustled into my room without even knocking. "Rise and shine," she said, surveying my mess. She picked up a pair of shorts and a T-shirt and folded them against her chest.

"I'm not ready to get out of bed yet," I told her, turning over. I felt mad at her, like I had been tricked. She should have told me. She should have warned me. My whole life, I had never known my mother to lie. But she had. All those times when they'd supposedly been shopping, or at the museum, on day trips—they hadn't been any of those places. They'd been at hospitals, with doctors. I saw that now. I just wished I had seen it before.

My mother walked over to me and sat on the edge of my bed. She scratched my back, and her fingernails felt good against my skin. "You have to get out of bed, Belly," she said softly. "You're still alive and so is Susannah. You have to be strong for her. She needs you."

Her words made sense. If Susannah needed me, then that was something I could do. "I can do that," I said, turning around to look at her. "I just don't get how Mr. Fisher can leave her all alone like this when she needs him most."

She looked away, out the window, and then back down at me. "This is the way Beck wants things to be. And Adam is who he is." She cradled my cheek in her hand. "It's not up to us to decide."

Susannah was in the kitchen making blueberry muffins. She was leaning up against the counter, stirring batter in a big metal mixing bowl. She was wearing another one of her cotton housedresses, and I realized she'd been wearing them all summer, because they were loose. They hid how thin her arms were, the way her collarbone jutted up against her skin.

She hadn't seen me yet, and I was tempted to run away before she did. But I didn't. I couldn't.

"Good morning, Susannah," I said, and my voice sounded high and false, not like my own.

She looked up at me and smiled. "It's past noon. I don't think it counts as morning anymore."

"Good afternoon, then." I lingered by the door.

"Are you mad at me too?" she asked me lightly. Her eyes were worried, though.

"I could never be mad at you," I told her, coming up behind her and putting my arms around her stomach. I tucked my head in the space between her neck and her shoulder. She smelled like flowers.

She said, still in her light voice, "You'll look after him, won't you?"

"Who?"

I could feel her cheeks form into a smile. "You know who."

"Yes," I whispered, still holding on tight.

"Good," she said, sighing. "He needs you."

I didn't ask who "he" was. I didn't need to.

"Susannah?"

"Hmm?"

"Promise me something."

"Anything."

"Promise me you'll never leave."

"I promise," she said without hesitation.

I let out a breath, and then I let go. "Can I help you with the muffins?"

"Yes, please."

I helped her make a streusel topping with brown sugar and butter and oats. We took the muffins out of the oven too early, because we couldn't stand to wait, and we ate them while they were still steaming hot and gooey in the middle. I ate three. Sitting with her, watching her butter her muffin, it felt like she'd be there forever.

Somehow we got around to talking about proms and dances. Susannah loved to talk about anything girly; she said I was the only person she could talk to about those kinds of things. My mother certainly wouldn't, and neither would Conrad and Jeremiah. Only me, her pretend-daughter.

She said, "Make sure you send me pictures of you at your first big dance."

I hadn't gone to any of my school's homecomings or proms yet. No one had asked me, and I hadn't really felt like it. The one person I wanted to go with didn't go to my school. I told her, "I will. I'll wear that dress you bought me last summer."

"What dress?"

"The one from that mall, the purple one that you and Mom fought over that time. Remember, you put it in my suitcase?"

She frowned, confused. "I didn't buy you that dress. Laurel would've had a fit." Then her face cleared, and she smiled. "Your mother must have gone back and bought it for you."

"My mother?" My mother would never.

"That's your mother. So like her."

"But she never said . . ." My voice trailed off. I hadn't even considered the possibility that it had been my mother who'd bought it for me.

"She wouldn't. She's not like that." Susannah reached across the table and grabbed my hand. "You're the luckiest girl in the world to have her for a mother. Know that."

The sky was gray, and there was a chill in the air. It would rain soon.

It was so misty out that it took me a minute to find him. I finally did, about half a mile down. It always came back to the beach. He was sitting, his knees close to his chest. He didn't look at me when I sat down next to him. He just stared out at the ocean.

His eyes were these bleak and empty abysses, like sockets. There was nothing there. The boy I thought I knew so well was gone. He looked so lost sitting there. I felt that old lurch, that gravitational pull, that desire to inhabit him—like wherever he was in this world, I would know where to find him, and I would do it. I would find him and take him home. I would take care of him, just like Susannah wanted.

I spoke first. "I'm sorry. I'm really, really sorry. I wish I had known—"

"Please stop talking," he said.

"I'm sorry," I whispered, starting to get up. I was always saying the wrong thing.

"Don't leave," Conrad said, and his shoulders collapsed. His face did too. He hid it in his hands, and he was five years old again, we both were.

"I'm so pissed at her," he said, each word coming out of him like a gust of concentrated air. He bowed his head, his shoulders broken and bent. He was finally crying.

I watched him silently. I felt like I was intruding on a private moment, one he'd never let me see if he weren't grieving. The old Conrad liked to be in control.

The old pull, the tide drawing me back in. I kept getting caught in this current—first love, I mean. First love kept making me come back to this, to him. He still took my breath away, just being near him. I had been lying to myself the night before, thinking I was free, thinking I had let him go. It didn't matter what he said or did, I'd never let him go.

I wondered if it was possible to take someone's pain away with a kiss. Because that was what I wanted to do, take all of his sadness and pour it out of him, comfort him, make the boy I knew come back. I reached out and touched the back of his neck. He jerked forward, the slightest motion, but I didn't take my hand away. I let it rest there, stroking the back of his hair, and then I cupped the back of his head, moved it toward me, and kissed him. Tentatively at first, and then he started kissing me back, and we were kissing each other. His lips were warm and needy. He needed me. My mind went pure blinding white, and the only thought I had was, *I'm kissing Conrad Fisher, and he's kissing me back.* Susannah was dying, and I was kissing Conrad.

He was the one to break away. "I'm sorry," he said, his voice raw and scratchy.

I touched my lips with the backs of my fingers. "For what?" I couldn't seem to catch my breath.

"It can't happen like this." He stopped, then started again. "I do think about you. You know that. I just can't . . . Can you . . . Can you just be here with me?"

I nodded. I was afraid to open my mouth.

I took his hand and squeezed it, and it felt like the most right thing I had done in a long time. We sat there in the sand, holding hands like it was something we'd been doing all along. It started to rain, soft at first. The first raindrops hit the sand, and the grains beaded up, rolled away.

It started to come down harder, and I wanted to get up and go back to the house, but I could tell Conrad didn't. So I sat there with him, holding his hand and saying nothing. Everything else felt really far away; it was just us.

chapter *forty-four*

Toward the end of summer everything slowed down, and it started to feel ready to be done. It was like with snow days. We once had this great big blizzard, and we didn't go to school for two whole weeks. After a while you just wanted to get out of the house, even if that meant school. Being at the summer house felt like that. Even paradise could be suffocating. You could only sit on the beach doing nothing so many times before you felt ready to go. I felt it a week before we left, every time. And then of course, when the time came, I was never ready to leave. I wanted to stay forever. It was a total catch-22, like a contradiction in terms. Because as soon as we were in the car, driving away, all I wanted to do was jump out and run back to the house.

Cam called me twice. Both times I didn't answer. I let it go to voice mail. The first time he called, he didn't leave a message. The second time he said, "Hey, it's Cam. . . . I hope I get to see you before we both leave. But if not, then, well, it was really nice hanging out with you. So, yeah. Call me back, if you want."

I didn't know what to say to him. I loved Conrad and I probably always would. I would spend my whole life loving him one way or another. Maybe I would get married, maybe I would have a family, but it wouldn't matter, because a piece of my heart, the piece where summer lived, would always be Conrad's. How did I say those things to Cam? How did I tell him that there was a piece saved for him, too? He was the first boy to tell me I was beautiful. That had to count for something. But there was no way for me to say any of those things to him. So I did the only thing I could think to do. I just left it alone. I didn't call him back.

With Jeremiah it was easier. And by that I mean he went easy on me. He let me off the hook. He pretended like it hadn't happened, like we hadn't said any of those things down in the rec room. He went on telling jokes and calling me Belly Button and just being Jeremiah.

I finally understood Conrad. I mean, I understood what he meant when he said he couldn't deal with any of it—with me. I couldn't either. All I wanted to do was spend every single second at the house, with Susannah. To soak up the last drop of summer and pretend it was like all the summers that had come before it. That was all I wanted.

chapter *forty-five*

I hated the last day before we left, because it was cleanup day, and when we were kids, we weren't allowed to go to the beach at all, in case we brought in more sand. We washed all the sheets and swept up the sand, made sure all the boogie boards and floats were in the basement, cleaned out the fridge and packed sandwiches for the drive home. My mother was at the helm of this day. She was the one who insisted everything be just so. "So it's all ready for next summer," she'd say. What she didn't know was that Susannah had cleaners come in after we left and before we came back.

I caught Susannah calling them once, scheduling an appointment. She covered the phone with one hand and whispered guiltily, "Don't tell your mom, okay, Belly?"

I nodded. It was like a secret between us, and I liked

that. My mother actually liked to clean and didn't believe in housekeepers or maids or in other people doing what she considered our work. She'd say, "Would you ask someone else to brush your teeth for you, or lace up your shoes, just because you could?" The answer was no.

"Don't worry too much about the sand," Susannah would whisper when she'd see me going over the kitchen floor with a broom for the third time. I would keep sweeping anyway. I knew what my mother would say if she felt any grains on her feet.

That night for dinner we ate everything that was left in the fridge. That was the tradition. My mother heated up two frozen pizzas, reheated lo mein and fried rice, made a salad out of pale celery and tomatoes. There was clam chowder too, and half a rack of ribs, plus Susannah's potato salad from more than a week before. It was a smorgasbord of old food that no one felt like eating.

But we did. We sat around the kitchen table picking off of foil-covered plates. Conrad kept sneaking looks at me, and every time I looked back, he looked away. I'm right here, I wanted to tell him. I'm still here.

We were all pretty quiet until Jeremiah broke the silence like breaking the top of a crème brûlée. He said, "This potato salad tastes like bad breath."

"I think that would be your upper lip," Conrad said.

We all laughed, and it felt like a relief. For it to be okay to laugh. To be something other than sad.

Then Conrad said, "This rib has mold on it," and we all started to laugh again. It felt like I hadn't laughed in a long time.

My mother rolled her eyes. "Would it kill you to eat a little mold? Just scrape it off. Give it to me. I'll eat it."

Conrad put his hands up in surrender, and then he stabbed the rib with his fork and dropped it on my mother's plate ceremoniously. "Enjoy it, Laurel."

"I swear, you spoil these boys, Beck," my mother said, and everything felt normal, like any other last night. "Belly was raised on leftovers, weren't you, bean?"

"I was," I agreed. "I was a neglected child who was fed only old food that nobody else wanted."

My mother suppressed a smile and pushed the potato salad toward me.

"I do spoil them," Susannah said, touching Conrad's shoulder, Jeremiah's cheek. "They're angels. Why shouldn't I?"

The two boys looked at each other from across the table for a second. Then Conrad said, "I'm an angel. I would say Jere's more of a cherub." He reached out and tousled Jeremiah's hair roughly.

Jeremiah swatted his hand away. "He's no angel. He's the devil," he said. It was like the fight had been erased. With boys it was like that; they fought and then it was over.

My mother picked up Conrad's rib, looked down at it, and then put it down again. "I can't eat this," she said, sighing.

"Mold won't kill you," Susannah declared, laughing and pushing her hair out of her eyes. She lifted her fork in the air. "You know what will?"

We all stared at her.

"Cancer," she said triumphantly. She had the best poker face known to man. She held a straight face for four whole seconds before erupting into a fit of giggles. She rustled her hand through Conrad's hair until he finally wore a smile. I could tell he didn't want to, but he did it. For her.

"Listen up," she said. "Here's what's going to happen. I'm seeing my acupuncturist, I'm taking medicine, I'm still fighting this the best I can. My doctor says that at this point that's the most I can do. I refuse to put any more poison into my body or spend any more time in hospitals. This is where I want to be. With the people who matter most to me. Okay?" She looked around at us.

"Okay." We all said it, even though it was in no way, shape, or form okay. Nor would it ever be.

Susannah continued. "If and when I go off slow dancing in the ever after, I don't want to look like I've been stuck in a hospital room my whole life. I at least want to be tan. I want to be as tan as Belly." She pointed at me with her fork.

"Beck, if you want to be as tan as Belly, you'll need more time. That's not something you can achieve in one summer. My girl wasn't born tan; it takes years. And you're not ready yet," my mother said. She said it simply, logically.

Susannah wasn't ready yet. None of us were.

After dinner we all went our separate ways to pack. The house was quiet, too quiet. I stayed in my bedroom, packing up clothes, my shoes, my books. Until it was time to pack my bathing suit. I wasn't ready to do that yet. I wanted one more swim.

I changed into my one-piece and wrote two notes, one for Jeremiah and one for Conrad. On each of them I wrote, "Midnight swim. Meet me in ten minutes." I slid a note under each door and then ran downstairs as quick as I could with my towel streaming behind me like a flag. I couldn't let the summer end like this. We couldn't leave this house until we had one good moment, for all of us.

The house was dark, and I made my way outside without turning on the lights. I didn't need to. I knew it by heart.

As soon as I got outside, I dove into the pool. I didn't dive so much as belly flop. The last one of the summer, maybe ever—in this house, anyway. The moon was bright and white, and as I waited for the boys, I floated on my back counting stars and listening to the ocean. When the tide was low like this, it whispered and gurgled and it sounded like a lullaby. I wished I could stay forever, in this moment. Like in one of those plastic snowballs, one little moment frozen in time.

They came out together, Beck's boys. I guessed they'd run into each other on the stairs. They were both wearing their swimming trunks. It occurred to me that I hadn't seen Conrad in his trunks all summer, that we hadn't swum in this pool since that first day. And Jeremiah, we'd only swum in the ocean once or twice. It had been a summer with hardly any swim time, except for when I swam with Cam or when I swam alone. The thought made me feel unspeakably sad, that this could be the last summer and we'd hardly swum together at all.

"Hello," I said, still floating on my back.

Conrad dipped his toe in. "It's kind of cold to swim, isn't it?"

"Chicken," I said, squawking loudly. "Just jump in and get it over with."

They looked at each other. Then Jeremiah made a running leap and cannonballed in, and Conrad followed right behind him. They made two big splashes, and I swallowed a ton of water because I was smiling, but I didn't care.

We swam over to the deep end, and I treaded water to stay afloat. Conrad reached over and pushed my bangs out of my eyes. It was a tiny gesture, but Jeremiah saw, and he turned away, swam closer to the edge of the pool.

For a second I felt sad, and then suddenly, out of nowhere, it came to me. A memory, pressed in my heart like a leaf in a book. I lifted my arms in the air and twirled around in circles, like a water ballerina.

Spinning, I began to recite, "Maggie and milly and molly and may / went down to the beach (to play one day) / and maggie discovered a shell that sang / so sweetly she couldn't remember her troubles, and / milly befriended a stranded star / whose rays five languid fingers were—"

Jeremiah grinned. "And molly was chased by a horrible thing / which raced sideways while blowing bubbles: and / may came home with a smooth round stone / as small as a world and as large as alone. . . ."

Together, Conrad too, we all said, "For whatever we lose (like a you or a me) / it's always ourselves we find in the sea." And then there was this silence between us, and no one said anything.

It was Susannah's favorite poem; she'd taught it to us kids a long time ago—we were on one of her guided nature walks where she pointed out shells and jellyfish. That day we marched down the beach, arms linked, and we recited it so loudly that I think we woke up the fish. We knew it like we knew the Pledge of Allegiance, by heart.

"This might be our last summer here," I said suddenly.

"No way," Jeremiah said, floating up next to me.

"Conrad's going to college this fall, and you have football camp," I reminded him. Even though Conrad going to college and Jeremiah going to football camp for two weeks didn't really have anything to do with us not coming back next summer. I didn't say what we were all thinking, that Susannah was sick, that she might never get better, that she was the string that tied us all together.

Conrad shook his head. "It doesn't matter. We'll always come back."

Briefly I wondered if he meant just him and Jeremiah, and then he said, "All of us."

It got quiet again, and then I had an idea. "Let's make a whirlpool!" I said, clapping my hands together.

"You're such a kid," Conrad said, smiling at me and shaking his head. For the first time, it didn't bother me when he called me a kid. It felt like a compliment.

I floated out to the middle of the pool. "Come on, guys!"

They swam over to me, and we made a circle and started to run as fast as we could. "Faster!" Jeremiah yelled, laughing.

Then we stopped, let our bodies go limp and get caught in the whirlpool we'd just made. I leaned my head back and let the current carry me.

chapter *forty-six*

When he called, I didn't recognize his voice, partly because I wasn't expecting it and partly because I was still half-asleep. He said, "I'm in my car on my way to your house. Can I see you?"

It was twelve thirty in the morning. Boston was five and a half hours away. He had driven all night. He wanted to see me.

I told him to park down the street and I would meet him on the corner, after my mother had gone to bed. He said he'd wait.

I turned the lights off and waited by the window, watching for the taillights. As soon as I saw his car, I wanted to run outside, but I had to wait. I could hear my mother rustling around in her room, and I knew she would read in bed for at least half an hour before she fell asleep. It felt like torture, knowing he was out there waiting for me, not being able to go to him.

In the dark I put on my scarf and hat that Granna knit me for Christmas. Then I shut my bedroom door and tiptoe down the hallway to my mother's room, pressing my ear against the door. The light is off and I can hear her snoring softly. Steven's not even home yet, which is lucky for me, because he's a light sleeper just like our dad.

My mother is finally asleep; the house is still and silent. Our Christmas tree is still up. We keep the lights on all night because it makes it still feel like Christmas, like any minute, Santa could show up with gifts. I don't bother leaving her a note. I'll call her in the morning, when she wakes up and wonders where I am.

I creep down the stairs, careful on the creaky step in the middle, but once I'm out of the house, I'm flying down the front steps, across the frosty lawn. It crunches along the bottoms of my sneakers. I forgot to put on my coat. I remembered the scarf and hat, but no coat.

His car is on the corner, right where it's supposed to be. The car is dark, no lights, and I open the passenger side door like I've done it a million times before. But I haven't. I've never even been inside. I haven't seen him since August.

I poke my head inside, but I don't go in, not yet. I want to look at him first. I have to. It's winter, and he's wearing a gray fleece. His cheeks are pink from the cold, his tan has faded, but he still looks the same. "Hey," I say, and then I climb inside.

"You're not wearing a coat," he says.

"It's not that cold," I say, even though it is, even though I'm shivering as I say it.

"Here," he says, shrugging out of his fleece and handing it to me.

I put it on. It's warm, and it doesn't smell like cigarettes. It just smells like him. So Conrad quit smoking after all. The thought makes me smile.

He starts the engine.

I say, "I can't believe you're really here."

He sounds almost shy when he says, "Me neither." And then he hesitates. "Are you still coming with me?"

I can't believe he even has to ask. I would go anywhere. "Yes," I tell him. It feels like nothing else exists outside of that word, this moment. There's just us. Everything that happened this past summer, and every summer before it, has all led up to this. To now.

JENNY HAN has her master's degree in creative writing for children from the New School. She lives in New York City. This is her second novel.